Give yourself and your loved ones a perpetual gift of
healing love and lasting peace –

THE UNSEEN BLOSSOM

&

THE UNSEEN PATH

✦ R E V I E W S ✦

Review Rating: Five Stars

The Unseen Path *is a work of fiction in the adventure, interpersonal drama, and romance sub-genres, and was penned by author duo Zlaikha Y. Samad and L'mere Younossi. The sequel to* The Unseen Blossom, *we have previously seen our central protagonists Zuli and Lamar meet within a fantastical fantasy world where they searched for the mystical blossom that would bring healing to the grief of their nation. But back in the real world, Afghanistan is in deeper trouble than ever, and the new regime threatens to tear Zuli and Lamar apart forever. What follows is a poetically penned adventure tale that seeks to reunite hope and love even in the darkest circumstances. Adult and young adult readers alike have much to gain from the beautiful reading experience that author duo Zlaikha Y. Samad and L'mere Younossi have created. In this combination between reality and fantasy, there are many comparisons we can draw with our own lives and the oppressions and struggles which keep people apart and nations at war. Then, woven delicately into these poignant messages, we find the beautiful bond between the young protagonists Zuli and Lamar. One aspect I found particularly beautiful was the dialogue, which is laced with hope for the young people's futures but also discusses the harsh realities of life in a way that readers from all walks of life can understand. Overall, I would highly recommend* The Unseen Path *as a fantastic adventure novel with many hidden depths for its readers to explore.*

~ Reviewed By: K.C. Finn for Readers' Favorite

www.readersfavorite.com

§

The Unseen Path is full of stunning imagery and poetic language. It is a story of love and hope that blends age-old wisdom with modern themes. Readers will go on a journey through its pages that will make them want to take an actual journey to Afghanistan. A worthy successor to The Unseen Blossom. *A beautiful achievement!*

~ Deborah Ellis is an award-winning author, a feminist and a peace activist. Deborah penned the international bestseller The Breadwinner Trilogy, which has been published around the world in seventeen languages and debuted as a feature animated film. She has achieved international acclaim with more than thirty books to her credit. She has won the Governor General's Literary Award, the Ruth Schwartz Award, the Middle East Book Award, Sweden's Peter Pan Prize, the Jane Addams Children's Book Award and the Vicky Metcalf Award for a Body of Work. She has received the Ontario Library Association's President's Award for Exceptional Achievement, and she has been named to the Order of Canada. Read her entire biography: www.deborahellis.com

§

The Unseen Path is a perfect sequel to The Unseen Blossom. *The first book presented a dream, a beautiful vision of Ideal life, through the eyes of soulmates Zuli and Lamar. The second presents us with the exact opposite: the separation of the lovers, an armed invasion, and the specter of death. But in this setting, hope and faith light the way forward. This visionary story teaches that love and wisdom are key to raising individuals and indeed entire nations from the depths of despair to the height of glory. Superbly written, strewn with poetry and philosophy, and highly recommended.*

Saleena Karim is an independent researcher and writer from Nottingham, England. She is also a co-founder of the Visionary Fiction Alliance. Best known for the political biography Secular Jinnah & Pakistan, her novel Systems is inspired by a real visionary idea born in history.

www.visionaryfictionalliance.com/saleena-karim

§

The Unseen Path *is a novel that invites the readers to see the beauty of the Afghan culture, its people, and the collective humanity they share. It tells the untold stories of people who remain unseen as a result of violence and invasions. The two protagonists in the story, Zuli and Lamar are the symbols of hope, courage, love, and beauty who are personally affected by the horrific wars. Their love for each other and their country is inspirational and resonates with many who are affected by political conflicts and wars not at their own fault. The novel is filled with beautiful local and international poetry and words of wisdom which convey to the reader that when humans are hurt in one part of the world, the entire humanity suffers and affected in different ways. I highly recommend* The Unseen Path *as it is a story of truth, perseverance, courage, and hope.*

~ Dr. Nahid Nasrat is a Professor of Clinical Psychology at The Chicago School of Professional Psychology. Aside of her teaching and mentoring students over 17 years, she is a diversity expert providing training and conducting research on diversity issues in clinical psychology, including refugees' and immigrants' mental health. She was the recipient of the Outstanding Dissertation Award, which was a clinical manual for mental health professionals working with Afghan refugee women. Dr. Nasrat is the recipient of the following outstanding awards: Ignacio Matin Baro lifetime Peace Practitioner Award, the Anthony J. Marsella Prize, the (NCSPP) Diversity Award. Read her entire biography:

www.thechicagoschool.edu/faculty-finder/byname/nahid aziz

§

Where The Unseen Blossom *was a poetic fantasy,* The Unseen Path *brings its characters into the harsh world of war-torn Afghanistan; fictionalized but essentially recognizable. However, it weaves quotes from several religions, the poet Rumi, and others into its tale to take the story's meaning far beyond suffering and into a larger perspective of humanity.*

~ Ambassador Ronald E. Neumann is the author of The Other War: Winning and Losing in Afghanistan, and former United States Ambassador to Afghanistan. He is the current president of the American Academy of Diplomacy in Washington, D.C.

§

Another beautifully written piece of work, highlighting the writers' talents for the reader's enjoyment. A lovely story of escape in these uncertain times. I highly recommend you take a journey and travel through this poetic landscape of the authors' vivid imagination.

~ Hazel Houldey was born in Wales and has been writing poetry since childhood. She is the author of Dusting A Rainbow To Paint A Carousel, Are There Really Tigers In Tiger Bay, and her children's book is The Professor Of Wooden Birds.

§

THE UNSEEN PATH

a novel by

Zlaikha Y. Samad and L'mere Younossi

The Unseen Path

Copyright 2020© Zlaikha Y. Samad and L'mere Younossi

First Edition

ISBN 978-0-9981036-7-9   Print

ISBN 978-0-9981036-8-6   eBook

THE UNSEEN PATH

XII

‹ℓ A Letter Of Gratitude ℘

In January 2019, unexpectedly, a whirlwind of ideas started spinning in my head for a follow-up to *The Unseen Blossom*. To be honest, I tried to ignore these thoughts. After all, I was putting all my effort into promoting our first book, *The Unseen Blossom*. I realized very quickly that there was yet another miraculous occurrence upon us.

Once the storylines and paragraphs began to appear in my mind's eye, I was left with no choice but to follow my instincts. Believe me, as I began writing, I realized stopping was an impossibility. *The Unseen Path* was finished on a Sunday, my birthday. Taken by surprise, with tears streaming down my face, I walked outside. I looked skyward to the clear blue expansion above and thanked God for such a kind gift.

I wholeheartedly thank Madee, my talented, kind-hearted, hardworking, and beautiful daughter. She remained by my side as she did during the creation of *The Unseen Blossom*. She helped with rounds of brainstorming, editing, and proofreading while on break from college, and during the stay-at-home orders related to the COVID-19 pandemic. There are no words for me to properly express my thanks to my lovely Madee.

Equally and wholeheartedly, I thank Wais Sadozai for his continued support with the technical and administrative aspects of book creation. I will forever be grateful.

Above all, I sincerely extend my endless thanks to my co-author, L'mere Younossi, for his support. He remains the spiritual inspiration for the creative writings throughout the novel. I am thankful.

Last, but not least, L'mere and I sincerely thank everyone who helped in the editing and proofreading of this book.

Love, light, and luck are our wishes to you and yours.

❧ Contents ☙

A Letter Of Gratitude XIII

CHAPTER ONE 1
☙ *The Second Encounter*

CHAPTER TWO.. 7
☙ The *Following Day*

CHAPTER THREE..................................... 17
☙ *Two Hearts Connected as One*

CHAPTER FOUR 31
☙ The *Finest Day*

CHAPTER FIVE 51
☙ Cherished *Memories*

CHAPTER SIX 69
☙ Liberty *and Dignity*

CHAPTER SEVEN..................................... 87
☙ Princess Zuli

CHAPTER EIGHT 99
☙ Uprooted

CHAPTER NINE 121
☙ The *Harsh Realties*

CHAPTER TEN 143
☙ Unexpected *Miracles*

CHAPTER ELEVEN 155
☙ The *Queen and King of Hearts*

CHAPTER TWELVE.................................. 195
☙ The *Unseen Path*

A Note To Our Dear Readers 201

My Dearest Brother 202

About The Authors 205

Resources 208

The End 209

§

"I fear God the most, but after Him I fear those who do not fear Him."

~ Saadi

§

§

"Whoever does an atom's weight of good, will see it, And whoever does an atom's weight of evil, will see it."

* The Holy Qur'an *

Surah Az-Zalzalah [99:7-8]

(The Quake)

§

§

"For those who exalt themselves will be humbled, and those who humble themselves will be exalted."

* The Holy Bible *

Matthew [23:12]

§

xx

CHAPTER ONE
The Second Encounter

T here he stood, motionless. Round about him, the hustle and bustle slowed to a halt, and the sounds ever so leisurely faded away. He was disoriented. In an attempt at regaining his composure, he focused on the moving figure. As the distance grew between them, he watched as her wavy hair swayed, the gentle breeze twirling and twisting long strands into vine-like braids. The restless wind made its way toward him, mingling with his long curly hair until his eyes were obscured by the tangled mess. He swept his hair back, focusing on that girl. She ran into him and, without wasting any time, took off even faster.

Before Lamar was out of earshot, she spoke, and he held tight to every word: "My name is Zuli and I am sorry for tripping you! I do hope you are not hurt too badly. Since my mother is very strict, I cannot be late for supper at eight. I shall return tomorrow to check on you. Meet me under the fig tree in the Garden of Ali Mardan. Forget me *not*."

She who shared her name with him was gone, yet her voice still rang in his ears. As she sped off, the street filled with floating dirt particles. Her footprints remained after she disappeared from his searching sight.

Pushing all thoughts to the back of his mind, he decided to follow her. If he remained in his stunned state, it would be impossible to pinpoint her within the maze of streets. Lamar, a fast runner himself, sprinted after Zuli in a desperate attempt to reach her. He tracked her footsteps until he reached the Kabul river and had to cross the shaky bridge. Zuli had suddenly faded from sight. The Kabul sky brimmed with gold, exposed to the onlookers, as Lamar turned in circles amid an unfamiliar crowd.

Disappointed, Lamar's gaze shifted to the delicate, vibrant laces he still clutched in his firm grasp. Within them was his late grandfather's silver-tipped tree branch. All at once, he started to hear an inundation of voices as colorful images began to replay in his mind.

Lamar headed towards his home, shutting out any and all surrounding sounds so he could focus on the inner noises rampaging through him. He was not sure what was happening to him, but he knew that it must have something to do with her – Zuli. Who was she? Why did she want to meet him tomorrow? She could have picked anywhere, but she chose The Garden of Ali Mardan, the only place where he felt rooted and at peace. He rounded the corner and saw a figure run farther down the path in a frenzied rush. Lamar picked up his pace, eyes glued on his target.

Zuli took a sudden left turn towards an unfamiliar neighborhood. This area was less crowded. Lamar usually avoided this side of town, but occasionally he would pass by the castle's façade. From afar, he would observe the guards who stood watch over the majestic beauty in the middle of town. The fortified walls separated the king's abode and all its majesty from the quotidian life of his people.

Zuli nearly outpaced Lamar as she turned right, then right again, then left. He lost count, but she took another detour. She made another left turn and further up the street, she walked up to the king's palace. Lamar peered around the corner, hiding behind the crumbling remains of a brick structure.

As if by second nature, she casually moved to open the back entrance, but the door was locked. She briefly scanned her surroundings before rapping the door four times. With no time wasted, the door opened wide enough for her to slip through, out of Lamar's sight.

His heart sank as he weighed his options. No commoner in their right frame of mind would dare to approach the palace door. What would happen if he knocked on the door four times? What harm could he do? Would they open the door? If so, would he be arrested on the spot for trespassing?

As always, he was curious, and it was this curiosity that got the best of him throughout his childhood. He realized that, perhaps, it was better not to get arrested on the brink of the evening. Maybe he would get himself detained tomorrow! He would come back to see who and what was behind that door.

Indeed, it was a fine idea.

CHAPTER TWO
The Following Day

L amar reached his shoe repair shop and headed upstairs to his bedroom, a simple room with cracked old walls. Once painted stark white, the walls had become a less-than-ideal smoky gray. A fan was installed in the middle of the ceiling. He turned it on only in the most stifling heat. At high speeds, the fan let out a whistle much like the unpleasant mumble of a pitchy flute.

His most-used pieces of furniture included his wobbly chair and matching wooden desk, the same set that had long ago sat in his father's room. Yet, his most valuable possession was his extensive collection of books.

Lamar was, in his own right, a businessman. After all, he earned a living and paid taxes, as did all the other entrepreneurs. He assured himself that in the near but unforeseen future, he would reap the rewards of an economic empire by producing quality products for worldwide consumption. The proud seal on each product would read, "Made in Afghanistan, with perpetual love."

An extreme state of fatigue consumed Lamar's last bit of energy. He could only bring down the wooden box from the top shelf of his closet, remove the silver-tipped tree branch from the inner pocket of his jacket, and place the branch inside the box. This time, he tucked away the box under his bed.

He lay on his back, pressed into his tattered mattress, with the voice of the girl he pursued to the back of the king's palace still echoing in his mind, and he slowly drifted off.

Over the Kabul mountaintops, the sun rose to wake the entire nation. It was a bright, cloudless day – the sky a refined sapphire. The early morning prayers echoed from the mosques' minarets both near and far. That was the exact time Lamar awoke. He took a deep breath, filling his lungs with the crisp morning oxygen.

Unexpectedly, images began to materialize right before his eyes. He could see a brilliant sun, which was suddenly replaced by an expansion of flickering stars. His heart was pumping erratically. He studied the palms of his hands – they were clammy. *Maybe I took in too much air at once*, Lamar thought. Still, one after another, more images overwhelmed him. He felt a hand reach out and forcefully pull him to the ground. He briefly saw Zuli's face. Out of nowhere, the mouthwatering scent of lemons wafted through the open window, and Lamar was transported to a memory of eating lemons under a lemon tree.

He closed the window and, disorientated by the images, he climbed back into bed. *I must not have slept too well,* he contemplated. It was too early to do anything or go anywhere. There were no customers yet and few shoes left to repair. What time was he to meet Zuli? *Oh, dear Lord, what time should I be there? Maybe I should go right now and wait,* he thought. At least, he knew she had a suppertime curfew at eight o'clock sharp. He tried to imagine how grand the palace's interior must be. The food was probably always served piping hot, the drinks sparkling and sweet. Lamar missed his favorite chef's most exquisite cuisines – his mother's homemade meals.

Hunger, the most compelling of animal instincts. Lamar was famished. He got up and made breakfast. Usually, he prepared a platter of sunny side up eggs, onions, fresh tomatoes, spicy red peppers, and freshly baked bread. Today, he settled on a few bites of day-old bread topped with sour cherry jam and a cup of hot black tea with two spoonsful of honey and a dash of milk. He preferred honey over sugar.

Every morning, Lamar began his days by buying bread from the not-so-friendly baker across the street. He never figured out why the baker had a furrowed brow and a look of disdain tattooed across his face. Perhaps, it was the heat from the tandoor, the scorching dugout oven deep in the ground. As a matter of fact, Lamar had never seen the man's face because he wrapped any exposed skin in cloth to protect him from burns.

It never ceased to amaze Lamar how the baker and his assistants avoided falling into the makeshift earthy oven when they reached inside and slapped the freshly made dough on the hole's concave sides. The baker took the round dough in one hand, dipped his other hand in flour, and began to shape the dough into a long, thin oval. Afterwards, he tossed it to his unfriendly boss. Then he bent down and stuck the bread into the oven's interior walls to bake. When the bread was perfectly crispy, he used a two-pronged metal fork to remove his golden masterpiece. He always sprinkled black cumin seeds on the *naan* before it was taken to the front of the bakery and placed on top of the pile for sale.

After much deliberation, Lamar decided not to stake out the king's palace. Instead, he headed directly to the garden. No one was there. He walked around the lush fig tree and looked up at its branches reaching far into the receptive and infinite sky.

He brushed a fingertip against the trunk and was drowned by waves of increasingly familiar, yet unusual, overlapping images. At once, Lamar pulled away from the tree.

With both hands, he held his head, closed his eyes, and reopened them. He blinked several times to make sure that he was not dreaming. Yes, he was wide-awake. As though being replayed on a theater screen, he envisioned a rock speaking to him. Then, he saw a butterfly wink and disappear. He saw ponds filled with water lilies. Then, he flew on the wings of a dove. Dazed, Lamar hesitantly walked away from the tree. He rested at his usual spot behind a curved wall where he could see the entire garden while still hidden from sight.

Distancing himself from the fig tree did not help with the dizzying visions. His sense of familiarity slowly dissipated. The more he continued to dig deeper into his memories, the more he confirmed that these visions were not dreams and were rather unmistakably genuine. Like an out-of-body experience, he saw himself shaking the fin of a tiny grinning fish that spoke eloquent words of wisdom. He heard a bird's calling in the distance and felt a phantom weight atop his left shoulder. Yet, nothing was there. *Well,* he thought to himself, *I am officially losing my mind.*

The hours inched by at the pace of a motionless snail. He stood up from behind the wall and saw a shadow creep over the mossy ground. It was time. His knees went weak and his heart leapt to his throat. He crouched down so she would not see him. He noticed that in her left hand, she held the same notebook from yesterday. He wondered what he should do. Should he casually walk up to her? He decided to remain out of view and observe.

Sure enough, just as he did, she went right up to the fig tree. She walked around, looked straight up at the sky, and reached out to touch the tree trunk. Not even a split second after the tips of her fingers met the tree, did she let out a gasp. She stepped away from its enormous trunk. It was as though she had been bitten or an electrical current had gone through her fingers to her entire body. She looked down at her hand with puzzlement then surveyed the surrounding grounds. Lamar sneaked around the garden's wall and pressed against the stone. He wanted to casually reenter through the front gates, so he could display the appropriate etiquette and be timely.

No one was in the garden, especially not the tall young man Zuli had encountered yesterday. *What if he does not show up?* she thought to herself, feeling anxious. Her hand still buzzed, as though recovering from the shock of a barbed wire or electric socket.

She turned back to the tree and was consumed by abstract impressions of tulips, roses, and pearls. Sunflowers swayed in the corners of her mind. She saw herself covered in pure rainbows, then sitting in a purple tunnel. A black horse bowed to her. She felt as though she had been lifted and was floating in midair. Even though it was clearly daytime, she envisioned a darkened sky lit up by a bright moon.

Zuli tentatively touched her face. How could it feel both tear-soaked and completely dry? Her feelings enveloped her with an undeniable premonition. "How surreal," she muttered under her breath.

She realized that she forgot an important factor of identification in yesterday's momentary exchange. *Why did I not ask what his name was?* Just then, she spotted the slender, sun-kissed man with thick highlighted hair make his way through the entrance with ease. He locked eyes with her. She felt his gaze penetrate her physical being and lock onto her heart, which beat at an irregular and accelerated pace.

He walked straight up to her and began to extend his hand before quickly changing his mind. He pulled his hand away and placed it on his chest:

"My name is Lamar. I hope I did not keep you waiting for too long, Zuli. I have been visiting this garden since I was just a child. It appears that you, too, are familiar with the grandest of all trees. It's a most glorious day, is it not?" *Good Lord*, he thought to himself. He could not help his incessant rambling. Before he could stop, he began to repeat himself, "It's a glorious day..." To his relief, she responded before he could finish his sentence.

Zuli extended her hand to him. He wasted no time, grabbing it with a strong grip. As soon as he took her hand in his, she firmly shook it and let go as if his hand was a lump of burning coal.

Yesterday, when Lamar had followed her, she had sped away while holding her notebook in front of her face. He assumed she was blocking out the heat of the sun or shielding her face from the world. Today, Zuli wore an indigo hat, similar to the kind cricket players wore, with a long peak that hid her eyes and shielded the rest of her face. She removed it and combed through her wavy hair with her fingers.

Zuli took a wavering breath. "It's a pleasure to meet you, Lamar. Thank you for meeting me today. I wanted to apologize to you face-to-face for knocking you off your feet yesterday. Frankly, I didn't think you would show up. I appreciate your thoughtfulness and that you took time out of your busy schedule to meet me on such a short notice."

"Well, Zuli, I'm only here for my medical compensation! I was gravely injured from yesterday's fall," Lamar joshed.

He saw the slightest trace of a smile pass over her lips. Lamar was most satisfied by her subtle reaction. On top of being both clumsy and pretty, she had a good sense of humor too. Besides, she was quite articulate and poised for a maid. After all, why else would she have entered from the back door of the palace? As the housekeeper's daughter, she probably had no choice but to work there.

After they shook hands and she pulled away from his warm grip, Zuli gently touched her own hand. He felt familiar. She turned away from Lamar's smoldering gaze and faced the fig tree. She did not want him to see her blush.

Zuli kept her attention on the tree. "I'll be more than happy to pay for all the medical expenses that you've incurred. Plus, I would most certainly confess in court should you decide to sue me on the basis of bodily harm! On another note, you're right about my familiarity with this garden. My father used to bring me here. Under this fig tree, we've had many heartfelt and profound discussions on an array of topics from poetry to politics. His wise teachings shall remain with me for a lifetime. As I think back, I realize that his teachings allowed me to stand upon a most strong foundation. They were designed to define and enlighten my core identity." Zuli looked up, still speaking to Lamar, "It's such a grand tree, is it not?"

"Indeed, it is outstanding," Lamar answered. Zuli turned away from the tree, faced him, and suggested that they walk around the garden towards the flowerbeds.

After hours of pacing and conversing about anything and everything, they returned to their original spot, right under the fig tree. It felt as though they had spent mere minutes together. Surprisingly, the more they walked and talked, the more comfortable they grew side by side. Words traveled back and forth between them, pouring out with no hesitation. Humor was the highlight of their conversations, peppered with smiles and giggles. They could not have asked for a more perfect afternoon. Zuli was most relieved that it was a weekday, so nobody was in the garden. People were just getting off work and heading home to the next stage of their day.

"Let's sit here and rest a bit before we leave," Lamar suggested.

They stopped at the tree and sat on the blanket of fresh grass covering the ground. Lamar waited for her to sit before he sat himself down next to her. They were shoulder to shoulder with just a little space between them to avoid being tightly pressed together. Relaxed, they simultaneously took a deep breath and leaned into the trunk of the fig tree.

A sudden deafening silence surrounded them. Not even the birds twittered as usual.

Out of nowhere, Zuli let out a high-pitched screech; Lamar firmly grabbed onto her arm as he, too, gasped out of sheer shock.

CHAPTER THREE
Two Hearts Connected As One

They felt as though the tree was going to give way and that they were going to fall straight into the earth. Immediately, a bubbling sense of power erupted from beneath the ground. A startling shock went through their entire bodies. Without realizing it, the two strangers clung to each other. Suddenly, the bright day's hue darkened, and an array of moving images appeared as if on a screenless movie.

Without even looking at each other, transfixed with widened eyes, both Zuli and Lamar uttered the same single word: "Unbelievable."

Adir, the wise rock, greeted them with his welcoming smile. Rocks spilled from his mouth and dust flew all around. "Welcome back, my good friends. Do not blink. Do not speak. Just watch. At the end, you will not see me. So, once again, all is not as it seems. You are Ambassadors of Peace. Hold on tight to your memories. We are just one step separated, next to one another. No matter what, all paths will intersect in your world. I wish you a life of abundance, serenity, and peace. However, peace only comes to those who maneuver through the dark shadows of loss without ever letting their inner light burn out. This light must remain intact so that there will be a bright future for generations to come. If you wish for the cries of death to be drowned by the cries of birth and for peace to conquer hate, then your light must remain bright."

Adir vanished, out of sight.

The images began to form a twirling circle around Zuli and Lamar, enveloping them at increasing speeds. The mix of colors was dizzying, as tornado-like winds made the entire garden pulsate and sparkle. Their surroundings were bathed in a deep crimson light. Suddenly, everything came to a halt. Zuli and Lamar reached for each other's hands and interlocked their fingers.

In utter astonishment, they saw a familiar version of themselves projected before them. Sure enough, they had engraved their names on the massive rock, Adir. Then, they watched the very moment Zuli had been pulled through the fig tree. The two looked on as they had walked through the fields of tulips, and they had swum in the lily ponds. They watched as rose petals had filled the air and Sadaf the mother dove had carried them home.

Every little detail of their mystical journey through the magical gardens was retold solely for their eyes. Their previously repressed memories filled the crevices of their minds and reignited their unbounded connection.

The mid-air movie disappeared. Both Zuli and Lamar froze. Neither one was certain whether the other was still breathing. There was a long pause before Lamar turned to look at Zuli. He could see her eyes had welled up and her face was wet from tears. Each tear was as precious and perfectly formed as a pearl, the same pearls they had just seen floating under the lily ponds. *How incredibly lovely she looks even when crying,* he thought to himself.

Lamar was overwhelmed. His one and only love, Zuli, sat beside him under the fig tree. It occurred to him that the purest blossom, seen or unseen, was his love, Zuli. No other blossom matched her colorful soul, and no other blossom was as elegant. He saw that she was simply perfect.

Lamar, lost in the reality of what he had rediscovered, gazed deeply at Zuli and uttered his truth.

"Now it's clear that you're the light that shall make my days brighter. I'm closer to you than you are with yourself. When you truly look within, you'll always be with me. You're the mirror for all those who are lovers of love. You're the endless ocean of passion. I am filled with boundless affection for you. My truth radiates for you like gold under the blazing sunlight. How could I have ever forgotten you, my most special princess? I love you with my heart, mind, and soul."

Zuli and Lamar leaned forward with tearstained faces and kissed deeply, forgetting that they were unhidden from the eyes of the public in *their* garden. The society in which they lived did not allow for public displays of affection, even with one's spouse. Holding hands in certain parts of the country could be costly and life-endangering.

"Lamar, my darling love of my life. No wonder your touch felt so familiar and comforting. No wonder I just had to see you again. No wonder I barely slept last night. No one in this world knows of our devotion. Rumi said it best, 'The minute I heard my first love story, I started looking for you.'"

Quite untimely, the great Hafiz's poems came to her. To concentrate on Lamar, she tried to push away his grand words to no avail: *And for no reason, I start skipping like a child. And for no reason, I turn into a leaf. That is carried so high, I kiss the sun's mouth. And dissolve.* Indeed, she wished to skip around their garden and dissolve. Instead, she softly uttered, "The root of our love is implanted in this garden and beyond. If only we could go back to the magical gardens."

As she spoke her deepest truth, Lamar had both of his hands on each side of Zuli's perfectly shaped face. Through the tears of joy and pain, Lamar wished he could take her away from a life that prohibited them from being together. While she verbalized her feelings, he planted little kisses all over her forehead, cheeks, and hands. She was the face of all beauties. Lamar knew if the king and queen found out that Princess Zuli was in love with a man who had no family, no status, and no right to their daughter, they would ascertain that he be ousted from Kabul altogether.

After leaving the garden, they made sure to walk separately once back on the streets. Zuli went first and Lamar followed. The problem was Zuli was not sure where to go. If she returned home, could she smuggle Lamar into the palace? She was not too certain whether her nanny, Gulnar, would take such a huge risk to help her. Gulnar had been her only accomplice all her life, but this was pushing the boundaries to undeniably dangerous limits. She was prepared to take the risk and made a sharp right turn.

Lamar realized Zuli was leading him towards the palace. He began to feel uneasy. It did not seem like a sound idea, but he continued to follow in fear of losing her. He knew all too well that without Zuli, he could neither exist nor would want to exist. She was him.

Lamar hid around the corner so that whoever opened the back door of the palace would not be able to see him. He could faintly hear Zuli whispering with someone who stood in the doorway out of his view. Her tone and hand gestures indicated someone trying to both plead and argue at the same time. To his astonishment, Zuli waved him towards her. He wasted no time and rushed to her side. Her nanny had allowed him to enter the premises.

Zuli led him to a small room in the backyard. It was more than just a room. There were several adjoining rooms with small windows where Gulnar and her family lived. Her husband had passed away and she lived with her two young daughters. Not surprisingly, her daughters also worked in the palace. However, what stunned Lamar was the fact that the daughters were encouraged to attend school. Apparently, the queen wanted the two girls to study hard and eventually attend college. She wanted the sisters to rise in society and bring an end to servitude. This goal was far more forward-thinking than the Afghan societal norm and was exactly the lesson Zuli and Lamar learned on their magical journey.

Lamar could hear Adir's resounding voice, recounting the profound lessons he beheld about the secrets of the unseen blossom: *We are responsible not only to do good to ourselves but also to society. Yes, we must try to better ourselves to reach higher levels of being human. However, we must also be a stage for others to stand on and shed light onto the greater populace. The only means of ensuring perpetual prosperity for oneself is to lift up those around us.*

Soon after Zuli smuggled Lamar in the palace, she left him in Gulnar's room, promising him that she would return shortly. She was apprehensive, but there was no other choice than to leave him. She bent forward and placed a kiss on his face. Lamar noticed Gulnar and her daughters blush and avert their eyes. Seconds after the kiss was planted on his cheek, he found himself completely alone. The mother and her two daughters bustled away, getting right back to work.

Lamar was grateful to finally be left alone so he could gather his thoughts about the surreal events of the day. How bizarre it was that he was sitting in the servants' quarters of the king's palace. He could not wait until Zuli returned. They needed hours upon hours to decipher the miracles of their fantastical journey. There was so much to discuss and plan. Finally, his future was unfolding in the most promising way.

Gulnar returned and placed a magnificent platter in front of him. Lamar's eyes widened and the grumbling sounds of hunger amplified as he scanned the different dishes of food. He was not a big eater. However, this once he could not refrain from devouring it all. Although Lamar was ecstatic, he still felt out of sorts.

Sultan Walad, Rumi's son, had said it best: *The one made alive by God will never die. He lives through God and not through gold and bread.*

The last time he was served homemade food was by his mother. Before the war. Before he lost his parents. Before his home was taken, and before he was left behind, alone and desperate for a peaceful life.

Zuli rushed towards her bedroom to freshen up. She was late for supper. She scampered down the stairs, tripping over her own feet as she made her way towards the dining room. Her parents glanced up as she pushed open the door. They exchanged puzzled looks before her mother queried, "May I ask why you're late for dinner tonight?"

"Oh, absolutely no good reason. I had a little headache and dozed off. My apologies. Did I miss anything?" Zuli hastily replied and turned to her father, who was busy eating an eggplant dish topped with homemade yogurt and sprinkled with dried mint.

As he reached for another piece of bread, he looked in Zuli's direction and said, "We are going to meet for a private family discussion when dinner is done. I have to leave for a meeting afterwards."

Zuli's heart dropped to her stomach and she lost most of her appetite. She wanted to be far, far away from this gathering. She would rather be talking and eating with Lamar. Instead, she sat nailed to the seat of her chair, immobile, aside from a slight nod of acknowledgement.

Her father spoke with uncharacteristic hesitation and notes of unease, unlike his usual earnest conviction. Even though she wanted to excuse herself from the family meeting, she decided against it after her headache ruse.

She wanted to return to the love of her life, Lamar. She felt horrible having left him in the servants' quarters. He was a man of nobility. Above all, he was her prince, the keeper of her heart. He glorified parts of her soul. As Adir stated, they were soulmates.

However, she dared not say a word at the dinner table while her father talked about the unrest in the country. She could feel her mother's burning gaze upon her as she eyed her daughter closely. Zuli was sure that her mother was concerned about her obvious lack of appetite. After all, everyone knew that Zuli was not shy when it came to eating, at times asking for seconds and thirds.

At long last, the entrée portion of dinner was over, and dessert was promptly brought out from the kitchen. She wished they had skipped dessert just this once, but no. The doors swung open and out came her favorite dessert. She absolutely loved *ferni* – a delicate and sweet dish made from milk, cornstarch, sugar, rosewater, and cardamom.

She watched the cook make this dish each time. She waited until he poured the mixture onto a flat platter before she took the pot from him and ate whatever was left in it. With an artistic flare, the cook sprinkled powdered pistachios on the *ferni* after letting it completely cool off. Zuli always reached for a larger plate, one that put the dainty china to shame. She served herself twice as much, enough dessert for two.

To Zuli's relief, the queen stared at her plate of *ferni* with a raised eyebrow but did not say a word. Before touching their dessert, they left the dining room, walked to the family room, took their seats, and waited. Zuli took her plate with her, saving the heaping pile of dessert for Lamar. The phone rang and her father stood to go answer it in his study.

Zuli was just beside herself and, with this endless waiting game, her patience began to wear thin.

Gulnar entered the room. Zuli desperately wanted to race up to her and ask about Lamar's well-being during their time apart, but she restrained herself. She hoped that he had not left the palace and was still waiting for her.

Zuli locked eyes with her nanny and attempted some form of telepathic communication. With widened eyes, she was internally screaming, *please, tell me he is still here*. Miraculously, her nanny, who had raised her from birth, understood that inquisitive look in her eyes. Gulnar gave her the tiniest affirmative nod, confirming the very question that had yet to escape her sealed lips. Zuli settled back in her seat, letting out a heavy sigh of relief.

Just then, her father returned and cleared his throat with such authority that it reverberated within the room. Gulnar rushed out.

"Don't be alarmed, all will be okay," said her father, the king of the land.

"Alarmed?" her mother questioned. "Whatever do you mean?"

The king sat in silence and leaned forward in his chair. He abruptly stood up and began to pace the length of the room.

"Well, my dear, the war is about to entirely get out of hand. Reliable intelligence is reporting that our country, this beloved land of ours, will soon be invaded by foreign powers."

Zuli and her mother both gasped, uttering the same word with a whispered mumble, as if it burned their tongues to say it: invasion.

The king continued, "Yes, an invasion is inevitable. We don't know the exact time. I have to stay behind, but everyone else must leave the palace, and the country for that matter, within the next few days."

Zuli could hear her mother's incessant questions echoing around her. Her father attempted to comfort her.

Within those few minutes, Zuli felt an invisible force weigh her down, as though the sky was going to collapse on her. The weight of the world smothered her. She felt as though the ground beneath her was shaking as it had before her fall in the fields of tulips. However, this time, there were no flowers to soften her fall. She knew all too well that doomsday was approaching.

Her father's words were all jumbled together. Her brain rejected everything he uttered. Before she could hold back, she sprung out of her chair and the words leapt out of her chest. "No. I am not leaving! Never!"

Her parents were taken aback by the outburst. Zuli ran out of the room towards the servants' quarters. Without even bothering to knock, Zuli rammed Gulnar's sitting room door open with the entire weight of her body. It swung back with a deafening crack. Sizeable pieces of the wall behind the door broke and fell to the ground.

Lamar rushed to Zuli as soon as he saw the look of panic and fear on her face. He held her within his embrace. She was shaking.

Oh, how much more could she love Lamar? Her love for him was overwhelming, paining every fiber of her body. She could feel her body ache when they were separated. But this was the kind of pain that she welcomed. The feeling was utterly priceless. Zuli would never allow anyone to take her away from this comfort or from the love Lamar and she felt for each other.

"My love, is everything ok? Should I leave? Did you get in trouble with anyone?" Lamar's concerned and reassuring tone was exactly what she needed to hear. Her family and friends continuously assumed that Zuli was tough. Therefore, no one ever stepped forward to comfort her. She had learned from the ladies in her life that a strong woman never showed her emotions.

In fact, Zuli was everyone else's source of comfort. She was the counselor and advisor to those who shared their intimate, often painful, stories with her. She was the sound of reason for most. She made certain to be in the moment because she had, indeed, been given the gift of always being a great listener and healer. At times, even adults twice her age complimented her on her astute grasp of life at such a young age. Without a doubt, she was an old soul.

As Zuli hugged Lamar back, she apprehensively pulled away from his embrace. Honestly, she did not care that the people in the room were witnessing the display of affection. Zuli's words rushed out of her in the form of nonsensical sentences.

"Please, my darling love, calm down. Take a deep breath. I'm here for you," Lamar said in a most soothing tone.

Zuli took a couple of deep breaths and began again. "Now, keep this to yourselves. I just heard there's an impending invasion of our beloved land."

Zuli's emotions constricted her throat. No one spoke. A wave of dismay replaced Lamar's calm demeanor. She continued, "I wish I had more details to share with you. My father just told me that we will have to leave the palace within the next few days, but he didn't specify exactly when.

"Oh, Lamar, what will become of us? You *cannot* leave here. You could hide within these quarters. No one ever comes here. Stay here, alright? Promise me. Do you swear? Promise me now, please!" Zuli was beside herself with worry.

Gulnar spoke at her usual whisper, "Princess Zuli, what do you mean we have to leave the palace? Did His Majesty, the king, say anything about where we will be going?" She turned to her two daughters standing on either side of her. As a single mother would, she was trying to mask her fearful expression. She reached out and pulled her daughters closer to her, protectively wrapping her arms around their shoulders.

"I am sorry, but I don't know," said Zuli. "He didn't say when, where, or for how long. I'm sorry to say I didn't wait long enough. I bolted out of there to come here and tell you. All I know is that the evidence came from covert agents who work with our European allies."

Lamar led Zuli to a chair and sat next to her, keeping his composure so as not to upset Gulnar's daughters, who were already beyond frightened. "Foremost, my darling, you must remain strong. I will never leave you. Never. I have been closely following the news. Several diverse political groups are actively working against the government. Sadly, many close supporters of these groups come from within your family circle, and they are aggressively campaigning to overthrow your father. They've made deals with the worst kinds of enemies," Lamar said.

Exasperated, Zuli questioned, "What do you mean, Lamar? Who from my immediate family?" Zuli shook her head in disbelief, "I know my father has many enemies, but who would do so much damage not only to him, but also to the whole country?"

"I don't know how true the rumors are, however, I have heard that the king is being targeted by the former prime minister. According to political analysts, he has collaborated with both Afghan and communist political parties. His main goal is to topple the monarchy and establish a republic form of governance."

"My Uncle Malik?"

"Now, Zuli, it's all hearsay. Let's focus on what his Majesty just told you," Gulnar exclaimed. For the sake of the young ones in the room, she still made sure to appear calm. Truthfully, Gulnar was alarmed and shaken up by the news about the royal family and her homeland's fate. She was practically part of the establishment.

The king and queen were humble and viewed themselves as servants of the people. They served with an excellence that could only compliment such powerful, high-ranking positions. Gulnar could attest to their dutiful and faithful governance. The royals were most concise and conscientious. They knew that their love for their country was the bond of the heart, tied tightly to the heart of the land. It was not about the glory of their egos or the shine of the monarch's crown.

Invading another's land only represents the master plans of evil minds. However, an evil mind fails to understand that he unequivocally forgoes his fate to be penitent once he is in the presence of the One and Only. The devil meets his match on the day his deeds are unveiled and recounted, one by one. No dead root ever blossoms. No man who takes an ax to his own kind will ever walk on the path of glory or mercy.

Lamar did not verbalize his thoughts to the ladies, especially Zuli. He certainly did not wish to further worry her when she was still in utter shock about her trusted uncle.

With much conviction, Lamar spoke up. "Afghanistan's bordering countries are not well-equipped to invade. Deciding to do so could have significant repercussions. After all, like Emperor Augustus said, 'make haste slowly.' Any country that invades another is violating the sovereignties and human rights of all worldly citizens, not just those within the land that has been forcefully occupied. I place my bet on the Russians. After all, which other country or foreign force could be behind this political breach?"

"If that's the case," Zuli replied, "then we are all doomed."

CHAPTER FOUR
The Finest Day

B efore the midnight curfew, Lamar left the palace grounds to return home. He promised Zuli over and over again that he would be back in two days' time and they would reunite.

It pained Lamar to be separated from Zuli, who stood subdued and worried at the palace's back door. She watched him until he turned the corner and was out of sight. Before he left, they spent a few brief but private moments in a hidden corner of the backyard, away from Gulnar's family and the other palace inhabitants. They hugged each other, kissed passionately, and expressed how much they loved one another. Each touch brought them desperately closer. Lamar craved to take Zuli home with him. Zuli desired nothing more than to run away with Lamar and leave no trace of her whereabouts. However, her more reasonable conscience reassured her that they would be together again in a few short hours.

They tore away from each other's embraces and retreated towards the back entrance of the palace. Lamar slipped into the dark of the night.

Being alone was risky. The crowds knew that they should try to be in pairs or groups. The possibility of being apprehended after hours increased tenfold, especially if the nightly password was unknown. Of course, Zuli made sure Lamar knew the correct code word to avoid any unfortunate run-ins.

Thankfully, it was still two hours before the mandatory curfew. The law was established to protect civilians from different militia groups that roamed the neighborhoods at night looking to rob people, break into businesses, and commit other crimes. Thus, last year, Zuli's father and his cabinet placed this restriction on Kabul and the surrounding areas outside the city's parameters. Trained police and, at times, military guardsmen patrolled the main roads, back streets, schools, ministries, banks, and other public forums.

Zuli knew that being outside at this time of the evening was not a smart move. Most roads had no streetlights and would have been in total darkness, had it not been for the glow of the moon and stars overhead. Zuli glanced up and sighed in relief. There was a clear sky and a bright moon. The stars illuminated and covered the vastness above. Although there were no shooting stars to wish upon, and despite Lamar's promise to return in two days, Zuli made a wish to see him tomorrow and for all the tomorrows after.

As Lamar turned the corner and Zuli fell out of sight, he felt a drowning sensation deep within him. Tearing himself away from her felt like tearing off a limb. Lamar walked for almost twenty minutes straight, away from the palace and towards his home. He scoured every inch of the streets, searching for anything or anyone unusual lurking around. His eyes kept playing tricks on him. He saw shadows jumping out from every corner. Every tree branch looked as though it reached out for him. He was not his usual calm self. He felt an unfamiliar unrest within his inner core. Whenever Lamar felt this sensation begin to consume his inner peace, he took a few deep breaths to calm his nerves. Hearing Zuli announce that her family must move away from the palace was alarming enough to disturb an entire nation, let alone him.

He was so preoccupied by his array of thoughts that he did not realize that he was just a minute away from his home. He could see the tiny window that peered into his room. He was relieved to have made it home in one piece.

Earlier, he was unable to discuss the possibility of being able to see Zuli no matter where she moved to. But it was decided that Lamar was going to pretend he was Gulnar's distant relative. This plan seemed like the only way he could have direct access to the palace without taking any unnecessary and potentially life-threatening risks. Slipping in and out of the palace under the guards' noses and any other prying eyes was too dangerous a task to undertake. If he got caught, he could be placing an even heavier burden upon Zuli's welfare. She already had a constricted life within the boundaries of the palace, abiding by rules set only for a princess. Obviously, it took some considerable effort to convince Gulnar to help the two soulmates. Yet, after she heard what the risks of getting caught would mean for her and her family, she had no choice but to submit to their brilliant idea.

To get Gulnar's help, both Zuli and Lamar painted a vivid picture of what the queen's reaction would be. They described how the queen would probably place Zuli under house arrest in a windowless room that was covered in barbed wire. The door most probably would not even have a keyhole. Poor Gulnar looked from one face to the other and, without uttering a word, adamantly nodded and stepped away from the grinning lovebirds.

Lamar knew Zuli's mother kept a close eye on her. If only he could muster up enough courage to tell the queen that her daughter was in fact *his* queen. He could just imagine the queen ordering the palace guards to seize and banish him. So, for the time being, he was going to play his part as a relative, perhaps as a distant cousin. He was a good actor, so he looked forward to fulfilling this new role, all for the sake of love.

Lamar's appetite had been satisfied after having feasted on a most delicious dinner. He made a list of items he should be packing besides his clothes. He did not own much. However, he had some personal effects that he did not want to leave behind. From past experiences, he knew that when there were rumors of political unrest, he should always have a suitcase packed and ready to go.

The irony was that Lamar had vowed to never leave his beloved Afghanistan, even if it cost him his life. The moment he realized he could forever lose Zuli, however, those promises instantly went out of the window. He would follow her to the ends of the earth and back even if it meant leaving his motherland. For Zuli, he would sacrifice himself with honor and pride time and time again. He would give his life and would put his head down at her feet just to save hers.

Lamar got out of bed early. Even though he was set to visit the palace tomorrow, tomorrow was just too far away. He had to visit Zuli today. Besides, there were rumors of an imminent invasion. How many days before his land would be crushed under the feet of the ruthless enemy? There was no time to waste.

His first stop of the day was at the Kabul Bank. He withdrew every penny he had saved. A handful of pennies was about how much he had to his name. If he was prudent, the money would last him for the next few months.

His second stop was at a jewelry store. Pragmatic or not, he planned on coming here ever since they traveled in Mr. Matek's magnificent carriage to The Garden of Roses. He wished he could have made a necklace for Zuli himself, but there was no time now. The only remaining option was to buy a piece that was befitting for his queen, his most precious *jawhar, gawhar* – his very own *jewel*.

Zuli had admired the pearls under the lily ponds, specifically those floating in Queen Shahbanoo Sanam's pond. How could they ever forget their ride to the garden of roses in Mr. Matek's white, pearl-covered carriage. He remembered Zuli telling him that she did not wear jewelry unless it was for a special occasion. She often wore her favorite pearl necklace that was a gift from her grandmother.

A pearl would be perfect for Zuli. Her heart was just as pure as any pearl from under the lily ponds or the deepest parts of the ocean. Just like the moon, a pearl's surface also glowed and reflected light. In certain parts of the world, pearls were often thought to provide protection to the wearer. Lamar wished for her heart to be forever protected.

Lamar smiled to himself, wondering what Zuli now thought about a pearl's significance. After all, she was a walking encyclopedia. She enjoyed cutting him off to insert details he may have overlooked. There was a continuous war of words between them. One brilliant mind exalted the other.

The dark, dusty, and unkempt jewelry store was located near the bank. It was, indeed, the first time he had set foot inside a fine jewelry store. The owner completely ignored him, which he did not mind. He did not seem like someone who could afford a single thread, let alone what the usual clientele would purchase. Well, today, he had the power to buy whatever he desired. Despite the suspicious pair of eyes upon him, Lamar kept shopping.

As he passed one counter and did not see anything to his liking, from the corner of his eye, he saw a piece hidden in the far-right corner of the case. He stepped back and bent over the glass to see what it was.

"Sir, how can I help you today?" Lamar heard the owner say.

Lamar turned to face the older man, who was clearly uncomfortable with the fact that his customer was not a wealthy-looking chap.

Lamar was never perturbed by such arrogance. Instead, he rose above it. He smiled and asked if he could see the item hidden in the corner.

As the owner went around the case, he asked, "Sir, do you know exactly what you're looking to purchase today?"

"I do," Lamar replied.

The owner waited for more details but got nothing. He cleared his throat and looked at Lamar. Still, Lamar continued to study the case in complete silence.

From his oversized pocket, the owner took out a long chain. Attached was a big ring that held many smaller rings. From each small ring hung different sized keys. After thumbing through and trying each one by one, he figured out which key was for that specific case. Lamar remained painstakingly patient.

The piece which was handed to Lamar was perfect for Zuli. He could already envision her wearing it.

"How much are you asking for this piece, sir?" Lamar queried in a cool voice.

After an hour of negotiating, story exchanging, drinking a few cups of tea, and befriending Wasim, the owner, Lamar purchased the item which he had bargained down to a manageable price. Lamar had a knack for bargaining. He negotiated with booksellers, lumbermen, and farmers for both the chickens and eggs. He even bargained with the convenience store workers for a bottle of cold water. That was how his father did it, and that was how he would continue to do it.

Wasim was also pleased with his sale for the day. His business had gone down significantly due to the unrest in the area. People only came to his store if they were getting engaged or married. Everyone was afraid of the uncertainties in both Kabul and other city centers. No one wanted to risk making big purchases, so they had enough emergency cash on hand in case they had to flee another civil war. Thousands upon thousands had already left from different provinces by foot, on mules, or by paying exuberant amounts of money to be smuggled in cars and trucks across country borders.

Being a smuggler, covertly helping desperate people leave their beloved land to start anew in an unfamiliar territory, was a prosperous business. Lamar knew of so many Afghans who had left and taken residence in other countries worldwide.

There were heart-wrenching stories of how people were robbed, abandoned in the middle of nowhere, or worse – murdered. Depending on the season, people would perish either from extreme heat or from the freezing cold. Vehicles were pulled over and pillaged. Men, women, and children suffocated while hiding in car trunks. Women were raped, girls and boys were abducted, and men were shot point blank in front of their families. People suffering from immense pain risked their last breath to live under the banner of freedom. Simply, no matter how many ups and downs were on the path to freedom, human beings were born free and were meant to be free. Not even death was a deterrent.

Freedom is life, Lamar thought as he continued to listen to Wasim's plans.

"I haven't told my friends and customers yet, but I'm going to sell my store. Of course, I can only take a handful of my priceless commodities with me. I'll have to hide them well. Thankfully, I won't have to bury my precious cargo underground, like many of my fellow jewelers have. They are hoping to return to this country one day, but anything can happen at this point. I'm not sure if you're aware yet, but there are rumors circulating within society about a possible invasion. My most difficult task has been trying to sell everything else that I physically can't bring," he said. "God willing, I'm going to move to America. They say there are many fine jewelry stores there and that everyone is rich. Americans buy whatever they like, even if they don't have a need for it. I have a cousin who moved to Chicago. He always calls and tells me I should leave. Granted, he complains about the wind and cold, but he still has a business. He makes absurdly long sandwiches, cuts them into smaller portions, and sells each for a high price. Thanks to his hard work, he now owns two cars and lives in a three-story home. He told me Americans love to have a good time, eat, drink, shop, and are kind to all. That's what he said."

All this talk about Wasim's cousin in Chicago only reminded Lamar how poor he was. He did not even have two jackets to his name. He had one suit he had taken from his late father's closet.

Handshakes, hugs, and many thanks were exchanged between Lamar and Wasim. He placed Lamar's purchase in the best gift box he could find. He then stuck a small red bow on the top. Lamar slipped the box in the inner pocket of his jacket before leaving the store.

What a great day this was. It's going to get better once I hold my princess in my arms, Lamar thought to himself as he walked toward the Kabul river. There, across the shaky bridge was an exclusively male clothing store. He had to look sharp when he presented his gift to Zuli.

Lamar left his tattered clothes behind in the store. The shopkeeper was kind enough to help him select a pair of pants with socks to match, two different colored shirts, a jacket, and a warm sweater which he desperately needed. Last winter was unbearably frigid and it never stopped snowing. However, the fresh snow beautified everything and covered all surfaces from the mountains to the trees. The snow perfectly purified society's darkness and covered all its imperfections, while simultaneously causing hardships for the poor.

Most people, Lamar included, could not sufficiently warm up their homes during the winter. Those who lived in mud homes or tents were most at risk. Many children succumbed to death from the relentless frost. Lamar shivered profusely throughout the winter months.

He walked out of the clothing store and caught his own reflection in the large window of another store further down the block. *I look quite smart,* Lamar admiringly thought to himself. He was not preoccupied by outer looks, but just then he had to admit that he looked like a gentleman. Not a prince, but debonair for sure. He preferred real smarts in a man. He seldom befriended self-absorbed, flashy, and loudmouthed men. He had gotten into a few fist fights in high school with one particular student. He was from an affluent family, but lacked morals, bullied other kids, and was a complete showoff. Unfortunately, he also suffered from an intelligence deficiency. He failed the final year of school while everyone else graduated, with Lamar at the top of his class.

Lamar looked simply dashing. He was wearing dark washed denim that fit as if it was tailor-made. It was secured by a chestnut belt with a gold-brushed buckle. He wore a light beige t-shirt underneath a navy-blue cardigan with black and white detailing on the sleeves. Somehow, the salesperson talked him into buying a sporty vest of a deep chocolate hue, which brought the ensemble together nicely.

He had two more stops. He dashed home to drop off his new wardrobe and grabbed the tree branch wrapped in many magnificent layers of lace. He wanted to have it on him at all times, in case he could not return home in the imminent future. He was going to present it to Gulnar so that she would fully be convinced of their magical adventures. It was so unique that it would be impossible for her to liken it to any regular branch.

He then ran to his favorite flower stand. He crossed the shaky bridge, turned right. After a mile down, he turned right again. Further up the road was an older gentleman and his flower stand.

This old man was not only his friend but was also a close business associate with decades-old ties to his family. In years past, Lamar, either accompanied by his mother or on a solo trip, stopped to exchange pleasantries. His mother always sent him to buy flowers for special occasions.

Sakheegul grinned broadly when he saw Lamar approaching him. His eyes scanned Lamar up and down a few times before they exchanged greetings and embraced each other. Lamar never missed the opportunity to hug him. Sakheegul lived alone after his wife had passed. His children lived in Hazarajaat, located in central Afghanistan. Sakheegul always brought up how he missed his children and grandkids. With much regret, he explained how at this juncture in life he could not make such an arduous trip to visit his family.

Sakheegul had shaken Lamar's hand irritably, brought his face uncomfortably close to Lamar's, and blurted out, "Look at my gray beard. I'm an old man. My children think I'm still strong, but I'm not. They're busy and don't have enough means to travel themselves. Twice a year, I send them money to try and help out. What little I earn, I save half for them."

Sakheegul could never stick to one subject in a conversation. He commented on how good Lamar looked. As he grinned, he exposed his missing teeth. His two front teeth were missing with a single wide gap at the bottom.

"You must be in love, my son!" he exclaimed with glee, placing a hand on each of Lamar's shoulders and violently shaking him.

"That I am, my friend. That I am," Lamar laughed.

"Ah, the wonderful world of love. I was younger than you when I fell in love with BebeGul. One day we will be together again," Sakheegul sighed.

Lamar purchased an enormous bouquet. All the flowers of the magical gardens he had journeyed with Zuli were included in the arrangement. Of course, the more exotic flowers and plants could be found nowhere but in those gardens. Still, the bouquet was both colorful and unique since Lamar took his time choosing which flowers would bring back extraordinary memories for Zuli.

Lamar's last stop was at a bookstore. Here, he purchased a box of colored pens, a set of notebooks, and a Dari-to-English dictionary. He finally headed towards the palace and felt a deep yearning within his core. Such a surprise would surely sweep his princess off her feet.

While he was at the bookstore, he asked the clerk for a large bag, which he placed the flower arrangement inside so it would not be noticeable when he entered the palace grounds.

He knocked on the door four times.

He stood there, staring at the closed door, heart pounding. It did not open. After all, Zuli was not expecting him today.

He knocked four times for the second time. No one opened. Anxiety crept through his body. His heart rate shot up and he began to perspire through his new clothes.

He said a little prayer under his breath and knocked again. As he stood there, Lamar nervously checked the street to make sure he was not being watched or followed by anyone.

The lock clicked with an echoing reverberation that shook the door's wooden paneling. Lamar jumped back. The door opened just a hair, barely enough for him to see a sliver of Zuli. She opened the door wide enough for him to squeeze through. Within that split second, Zuli reached for his arm and pulled him in before hurriedly closing and locking the door. She put a single finger to his lips, and with her other hand, motioned for Lamar to follow.

Still carrying the two bags, Lamar followed without making a sound. She abruptly stopped in her tracks and turned to him. He put the bags down. In the same instant, they both rushed into each other's arms. They hugged one another with a passion that could only be found between soulmates. Lamar whispered into her ear so no one could hear his words but her.

"Oh, my darling, I missed you so much. I couldn't sleep. I felt so much pain in the seat of my soul and within each aching beat of my heart. Please don't ever leave me. Without you, I'm lost. I love you, my princess."

"I love you, my dearest and nearest. You're my prince, the keeper of my sanity. I missed you beyond all limits. I paced back and forth in my room all night. I wished upon the stars;

O' my wish is fulfilled. Once again, I discovered that you're my being – *you are me*. I cried and prayed to God to make the night pass and let the sun come out just a little quicker so we could be together again," Zuli whispered. She leaned forward and kissed Lamar.

Because it was still broad daylight outside, they had no choice but to stop hugging and kissing. The risk of being seen was not one they were willing to take.

The guards were patrolling elsewhere at the time. Nonetheless, they both had their story straight, and were ready to present Lamar's phony background to anyone who dared query. He was now committed to being Gulnar's distant cousin, one who had never, ever before visited!

After all, beauty tends to be amplified by an admiring glance, Lamar thought to himself as he watched Zuli's exuberant reaction to being handed the bouquet of flowers. She shut her eyes and slowly inhaled the fragrances.

"These are incredibly beautiful. They remind me of our walks through the gardens and meadows. We strolled up and down so many hills covered in flowers remarkably similar to what I'm holding. These are simply splendid. It's the most gorgeous arrangement I've ever seen but, of course, you look even more superb, my prince charming!"

Zuli and Lamar sat together in the nanny's room into the early evening. They were inseparable. This became more and more apparent to everyone who came and went from the palace's back door. Zuli took it upon herself to introduce Lamar as Gulnar's cousin. No one was given even a second to ask any questions. Polite handshakes and greetings were exchanged before the lovey-dovey couple would scurry off, leaving those around them baffled. They were sure everyone wanted more details, but Zuli was not having any of that.

"I will not waste our precious time answering nosy people's unsolicited questions," Zuli expressed. "You don't know this, Lamar, but I asked Gulnar to tell all the guards and the palace help not to talk about your visit. I want to be able to spend time with you without worrying about who is saying what.

You know how our culture is. They just love to gossip and make up different versions of a single story."

In his signature tone, Lamar said, "I understand, my darling Zuli. Don't stress yourself about what others may or may not say. Eventually, they *will* be talking. That's just human nature. After all, I'm supposed to be some distant cousin dropping onto the premises out of thin air. They see that I'm spending all of my time with you, not with Gulnar and her family."

Zuli looked at Lamar and they both burst out laughing.

Still laughing, Zuli mused, "I wonder what colorful thoughts are going through their twisted minds?"

"Why don't we drop the subject for now and let's get back to this," Lamar said before kissing Zuli.

While holding Zuli's hand, Lamar pulled her closer to his side and said with assurance, "This is the finest day of my life here in Kabul. Before we embarked on our mystical journey through the enchanted gardens, my life was dark and hope was nonexistent. I struggled through each day. Being spiritual, I usually have an unshakable inner strength, but I felt weak. My perpetual loneliness affected my jolliness and overall bearing. I saw my life and future falling apart, piece by piece. My grandfather always told me to have hope no matter what. Towards the end of his life, he often reiterated how solely the realities of pain were worthy assets for empowerment. Unexpected miracles stem from that magical glow we reap, from both harsh lessons learned and good deeds sent and received."

They sat outside under a tree near the window in Gulnar's room. Out of nowhere, they heard someone approaching them.

"It's almost dinner time, Princess Zuli. Where will Sir Lamar be eating tonight? Is he staying for dinner?"

"Thank you for asking, Gulnar," Zuli replied. "He will be eating with you and your family. I'll be joining you too. I will tell my mother not to expect me for dinner tonight."

Gulnar replied, "You *will?*"

"Yes, I will tell her that your *cousin* is visiting and that I have promised to have dinner with your family tonight. She can't object. She has no reason to do so."

"Of course," Gulnar quickly answered, throwing a puzzled, slightly concerned look at them both before rushing off.

"That went well, didn't it, Lamar?"

"I think so, my lovely. Let's just hope this change of plans doesn't raise any questions with your parents."

"It shouldn't. I have done this before at formal dinners when I didn't want to be around certain guests. I've had many dinners with Gulnar's daughters. Eating here is a much more relaxed affair."

Zuli left with a mission. She promised to be back shortly. She embraced Lamar tightly and lovingly whispered sweet words in his ear. She practically sprinted towards the front of the palace. Lamar wished he could have gone with her. He was sure the palace's interior was as grand as any king's palace would be.

He would ask Zuli to give him a tour when the king was out and the queen was taking her daily nap. *What an idea!* He could not wait to share it with Zuli over dinner. Of course, Gulnar would probably be pleased to help them.

On the contrary, Gulnar was not pleased.

"I will do no such thing. You know all too well that nothing remains hidden from the queen," she said adamantly.

Well, there goes Gulnar's help, Lamar thought to himself. She was not to be blamed. The poor woman was barely given any time to process Lamar's abrupt appearance. Zuli had briefly filled her in about their magical journey. Upon hearing such a fairytale, she thought the princess had completely lost her senses. On the other hand, she could not deny that Zuli and Lamar's connection was visibly unquestionable.

While they ate dinner, sitting side by side, Lamar noticed how Gulnar was studying them. Zuli urged Lamar to try the spinach dish. It was one of her favorites. Lamar crafted the perfect bite and hand-fed it to Zuli. She laughingly opened wide and nearly bit his fingers.

Gulnar easily deciphered that the two had not just met. Their kind of connection required time to grow into a full-fledged relationship with two people who had become familiar with each other. Gulnar had no choice but to believe them. How else could she explain their oneness? Surely, questions were circling in Gulnar's mind, ones Lamar was not looking forward to. He wanted to spend every second with Zuli. He wished to discuss their mystical journey only with her.

Too late. The questions came one after another. Gulnar, who had raised Zuli from birth, was like a mother to her. She had most definitely spent more time and given the utmost attention to Zuli than her actual mother had. The queen was often far too busy with working, hosting official gatherings, and traveling.

"Now, princess, tell me the story of this so-called magical journey. Did you say Lamar pulled you through a fig tree, the one in the Garden of Ali Mardan?"

Two hours passed as both Zuli and Lamar recounted their journey. They talked over one another, finishing each other's sentences, reminding each other of details the other had forgotten, mentioning the names of their mystical friends, and laughing at the funny moments they had shared. Gulnar served them green tea throughout but did not interrupt. She was at a loss for words and could not believe the two were speaking of the same details and memories. Lamar even presented her with the silver-tipped tree branch and she became completely overwhelmed with emotion.

The story drew to a close, as did any signs of light outside. It had quickly grown dark out. Gulnar could not believe that the journey to the unseen blossom was more than just a fairytale. She wept. She hugged them. She left them to go pray.

"Even if we sent down the angels to them; even if the dead spoke to them; even if we summoned every miracle before them; they cannot believe unless God wills it. Indeed, most of them are ignorant."
~ *Surah Al-An'am (The Cattle) [6:111]*

Lamar was always certain God had willed their journey. He had no doubts that Gulnar was a far from ignorant believer. After all, her motherly love for Zuli was neither less nor more than the love she had for her own daughters.

Barely a minute later, Gulnar returned to the room and said, "Lamar, you should stay here tonight. It's very late. You have just under an hour to get home. It'll be very risky to leave now. You can sleep in the guest room. The bed is comfortable and whatever you may need is at your disposal."

Before Lamar could accept or reject, Zuli sprang to her feet, hugging and thanking her. She even placed a few kisses on Gulnar's face.

"Princess, you can stay here for now, but you must be in your room by midnight. Your parents will check on you by then. Leave your bedroom light on so that they know you're in there. I don't want them asking me about your whereabouts, so make sure to leave the light on."

§

~ *The Qur'an*
~ *Ar-Rahman (The Beneficent) [55:19-22]*

[19] He has let free the two bodies of flowing water (salt and
     fresh), meeting together
[20] Between them is a barrier which they do not transgress
[21] Then which of the favors of your lord will ye deny?
[22] Out of them come pearls and coral

§

CHAPTER FIVE
Cherished Memories

"When you do things from your soul, you feel a river moving in you, a joy." ~ Rumi

Before it was time for them to part ways, Lamar presented Zuli with the ring.

Mouth agape, Zuli stared at him in astonishment and disbelief. She covered her mouth with one hand. Her eyes welled up with tears. Lamar always enjoyed her animated yet most sincere reactions.

Exactly as he had seen in the movies, he knelt, left knee on the ground, and held up the small box with both hands.

"Will you be the love within my heart? Will you be the star in my dark nights? Will you be the colors of my dawn? Will you be mine..."

Lamar fought back tears as Zuli herself bent down so they were at eye level.

"I will be your love forevermore. I will plant colorful flowers in our shared life's garden. I will always be yours, only yours."

A river of joy rushed through Lamar, the rapids of contentment lapping at the shores of self-doubt. So far, Lamar learned that richness was not a matter of material goods. Rather, a sense of wealth came from a soul's purity. That wealth blossomed from boundless comfort and hope. There was even a richness within pain. Pain itself was painful. Yet, its agony contained the hidden elements of a cure and the light of wisdom.

Lamar quoted Rumi as he adoringly looked into Zuli's glistening, teary eyes:

"Nothing can help me but that beauty. There was a dawn I remember when my soul heard something from your soul."

Lamar took the ring out of the box. Without hesitation, Zuli extended her hand. She giggled and pulled it back at once. Blushingly, she extended her left hand. He placed a tender kiss on her hand before sliding the ring onto her finger. It was a perfect fit.

"Zuli, dearest, under the gaze of our Creator, you are now mine and I am yours."

While the sweetness of their kisses lingered on her lips, Zuli waltzed back into the palace. She got to her room right on time, turned the light on, and threw herself on the bed. She studied her new ring. He clearly remembered her love for pearls. Unlike other jewels, which came from deep within cavernous mines, pearls were from the heart of the sea. Her ring had been selected by the man with a heart purer than a jewel found in the ocean's depths. Water had utmost significance to Zuli. It was purifying and gave life to all of nature, both plants and animals.

Zuli's new ring had three rows of small pearls placed in a symmetrical, circular fashion. The rows of pearls were connected by tiny gold bars. At the ring's center was a pristine spherical emerald, held in place by leaf-shaped golden prongs. It was a flawlessly stunning piece of jewelry selected by a perfect man. Zuli would forever cherish this lustrous and timeless symbol of their love.

Zuli arose before dawn. She washed up and threw on a comfortable, sporty outfit. She wore a high-collared shirt with long sleeves that ended in lace cuffs. Over it, she added a sturdy duster that hit right above her knees. She folded the jacket's sleeves to reveal the lace underneath. Zuli then tugged her tight-fitting dark washed jeans into her weathered lace-up boots. She gathered her flowing dark hair into a high ponytail.

She grabbed her notebook and hurriedly flipped through the pages until she saw the small green leaves, the ones she had picked from the green tunnel before they had gone to the garden of lily ponds. She left her room, first checking to see if anyone was in the hallway. She slipped downstairs without making a sound. Further down the hall and past her father's study, were the back stairs that allowed for her to leave the palace without a trace. She ran across the backyard towards Gulnar's abode. Sure enough, there he stood.

Without slowing down, she flung herself into his waiting arms. He lost his footing and they both almost crumpled to the ground. Instead, they struck the back wall, Lamar taking the brunt of the collision. They laughed out loud but quieted themselves so they would not awaken the palace residents. Holding hands, they vanished from open air to be alone in their secret hideaway.

"Time flies when love is in the air," Lamar said.

"That would be a great opening line to a poem," Zuli mused.

Lamar puffed his chest with pride, "Rumi would be proud."

Zuli was curious. "What would the next verse be?"

He started to retort, then caught himself, "It... it's a work in progress."

Later that day, after a scrumptious lunch, Zuli took Lamar on his official palace tour. In the early afternoon, she led him around the grounds and showed him all the palace's secret sites. The estate was lush green with an array of plants and flora, including well-kept rose bushes.

Her majesty had been napping, and the king had left the premises for a meeting with his cabinet. Since he would not return until dinner time, off they went.

Needless to say, Gulnar was a serial accomplice.

The grand palace's interior was exactly that – grand. Lamar tried to hide his unfamiliarity with such a lavish lifestyle. He was overwhelmed by room after room covered in exaggerated decorations of silver and gold artifacts. The painting-covered walls made it feel more like a museum than a home. Sofas, chairs, and tables of all sizes, with carefully picked fabrics and colorful patterns, were arranged in every room and hallway. Nothing he saw sat well with him. Zuli noticed his displeased demeanor.

"My darling, please don't allow all of this luxury to bring discomfort to you. Believe me, I am aware of exactly how you feel, and I know what is going through your mind. No matter where you look, royals and leaders live like this."

With a grandiose gesture, she pointed to the entire formal guest room and reassured Lamar about how none of the material *things* represented her family. She brought up their first encounter, when she asked him not to call her a princess. She was steadfast in defending her family's commitment to the welfare and safety of their nation.

"My father is a good man. All he has done is work tirelessly for the advancement of an impoverished nation. Just look..."

Lamar interjected, "My love, you don't have to explain anything to me. I'm neither in a position to judge, nor would I have reason to. I know how caring and giving you are. Obviously, your parents have the same values since they raised you to believe in ethical principles. The feelings rampaging through me have to do with the situation at hand. The country lives in despair and hope is a far-off light at the end of a dark tunnel that we may all have to, sooner or later, travel through."

They heard faint rustling from around the corner. Zuli ran to take cover behind a towering wooden bookstand and pulled Lamar by the forearm so he would follow suit.

"Come out from behind there, you two," sounded Gulnar's annoyed voice.

"How did you know that we were hiding here?" Lamar asked sheepishly.

"Oh, Zuli has hidden there since she was about five years old." Gulnar grinned as she warily eyed them both. "I'm going to go check on the girls quickly. Don't roam around for too long. The queen will soon be up from her nap."

The second Gulnar left the room, Lamar pulled Zuli back behind the bookshelf.

All senses vanished when the two lovebirds were in each other's arms. Time stopped ticking away. Yet, they knew that their palace tour had gone on for far too long already. They should have left the premises an hour ago. They hurried past the family room so they could reach the back door. As they passed the marble staircase that led to the palace chambers, they were confronted with their greatest fear.

"Zuli, is that you?" an authoritative voice asked from the top of the stairs.

"Oh my goodness," Zuli whispered. She held her forefinger to her lips, gesturing to Lamar to keep quiet.

She called out, "Yes, mother. I was on my way out. Did you need anything? I'm in a hurry."

"Is your father back yet? Where are you off to again? Come and stand where I can see you," her mother said.

Before Zuli could move, the queen asked, "Who is there with you?"

Zuli's face immediately dropped and a shudder went through Lamar. They stood in utter silence.

"Zuli," her mother called again.

Lamar nudged her to take a step forward. She walked to the foot of the stairs.

"Oh, good afternoon. You look well-rested. I'm on my way out, Mother. Gulnar's cousin is here and I was showing him the books in the library." Her mother wore an inquisitive expression, and her eyebrows shot up.

"I see. Please ask him to step forward. No need to be shy. Everyone is welcomed in this home."

Lamar shook his head violently, crossing his arms and stepping back. Before he could stop Zuli, she grabbed his hand and pulled him towards her.

They stood beside each other. He looked up the staircase and, at the very top of the landing, there stood the queen of the land. He placed his right hand on the center of his chest and bowed his head and upper torso. While he remained in that position, he hoped she would vanish completely when he straightened back up.

Zuli loudly cleared her throat since Lamar was frozen in place and had no plans to stand tall again.

Lamar got the message. He returned to his proper posture and looked up, only to be disappointed. The queen was still there.

Without blinking, the queen eyed him up and down, from his toes to his head. He did not even have time to fix his messy hair. Meanwhile, Zuli kept rocking back and forth on her heels, and a bead of sweat appeared above her brow. She was beyond nervous.

Surprisingly, her voice was cool and collected when she spoke, "Mother, this is Gulnar's cousin, Lamar. He has been staying with her for a few days. Remember? I mentioned him to you when I had dinner with Gulnar's family last night."

Speaking of Gulnar, Zuli saw her speeding down the hallway with a big grin on her face. She was ready to lead the two out of the palace before heading upstairs to tend to the queen.

When she saw them standing at the foot of the stairs, Gulnar halted in her tracks. The color had drained from their faces and their overall body language signaled nothing but panic and distress.

"Your Majesty, I see you have already met my cousin," Gulnar said as she bowed.

All the while, Her Majesty observed the two. Obviously, the queen noticed Zuli's flushed complexion and uneasy demeanor straightaway. The young man, Lamar, struggled to maintain eye contact with her. Even Gulnar projected an unfamiliar discomposure. There was no doubt in the queen's mind that something was not quite right, and she had, in fact, stumbled upon a cover-up.

"Gulnar, I am most pleased to have finally met your guest. Do set an extra place for dinner tonight. Lamar will be joining us."

"He *is*?" Zuli asked.

"Yes, Zuli. It is settled," Her Majesty said before she wished them a good day. While walking off, she threw an all-knowing look at the three of them.

They exited the palace in utter silence and crossed the lawn. Once they were completely out of sight, they all burst out talking. No one could understand the other.

"Look, you have no choice. It's too late, Zuli. You know once your mother makes a decision, it stands as such. So, I suggest you talk this over and make certain you have your stories straight. At dinner, keep the conversation neutral and say as little as you can. Let your parents do most of the talking. If the conversation gets personal, change the subject to a topic like economics or world politics. You know His Majesty enjoys such discussions. I need this job and if you mess up, I am not looking forward to getting fired. I hope I'm clear!"

It was almost time for dinner. Lamar had to look as presentable as possible. Zuli searched through the closet in the guest chamber and selected the perfect outfit. She decided to style him with a formal charcoal blazer and crisp white shirt. She helped him with a matching necktie, tightening it until he was practically choking. He grabbed at his collar and gasped for air. She giggled while loosening it.

"Can you hear my heart beating?" Lamar asked.

"I can't over the sound of my own."

As Zuli and Lamar waited, he placed her hand over his heart. Sure enough, it felt as though it was trying to leap from his chest.

The king and queen entered the dining room.

Over the course of one's life, love from the depth of the heart and height of the soul is a singularity that travels through time. As these words arose in Lamar's mind, he was certain that for the sake of love, his life had come to an end. Who could fool the queen and king? Not him.

Although Lamar's father was the descendant of lords, he had fallen in love with his mother, who was perceived as a commoner without any fancy titles or wealth. Lamar had recently realized and been utterly amused by this reversed fate. Now he was the commoner, and in society's eye, he was quite unsuitable for the princess. Yet, he vowed to defy such labels.

He was convinced that as soon as Zuli's parents realized true love had connected their one and only daughter, the princess of the land, to a shoemaker, the son of lords who were no longer alive to protect him, he would be imprisoned and punished. Prayers were in order!

Lamar was relieved to see how relaxed the king was. With all his power and might, he was the one to approach first. He warmly shook Lamar's hand as though they were old friends. He did not leave a chance for Lamar to bow, salute, or behave how he was supposed to in the presence of royalty.

A delicious dinner was served. The butlers suspiciously eyed Lamar, whose own eyes were sealed onto his plate. He wished he could take the necktie off. It was cutting off blood circulation to his brain. He could hardly focus on anything, let alone follow along with the conversation. Obviously, Lamar could not help but notice the class differences within the royal walls. There was no comparing his humble dinner at Gulnar's home to tonight's grandeur. *'In a country well governed, poverty is something to be ashamed of. In a country badly governed, wealth is something to be ashamed of.'* He kept Confucius' words hidden within his thoughts. He would never dare hurt Zuli's feelings with his painfully accurate observations.

Both Zuli and Lamar kept their mouths stuffed with food to avoid saying much. They knew to stick to Gulnar's suggestion. Zuli managed to divert the most awkward questions aimed at Lamar.

The only bit of luck they had at dinner was when a knock on the door consumed the king's attention. A package had been delivered and, thankfully, the king remained preoccupied with the responsibility of reading the official reports. Lamar assumed that the reports included updates on the civil unrest.

Teatime was the pits! The queen hurled personal questions at Lamar, one after another. *This is an absolute nightmare,* Zuli concluded. *Why didn't I anticipate such a calamity?*

Zuli could not keep up with the questions being fired at Lamar. After asking what he did for a living, her mother went so far as to probe whether Lamar was financially secure at such a young age.

The queen was positively baffled when Lamar replied, "Your majesty, I mend, arrange, and renew everything broken. It is the only security I give to others. It is the only richness I possess."

With every question posed, a most restless Zuli interjected her somewhat coherent thoughts into every painful answer.

"So, Lamar, how is it that you have never before visited Gulnar? After all, has she not been a part of your family for the past twenty years?"

The borrowed necktie felt as though it was deliberately trying to choke him, ensuring his inability to articulate a creative answer. Just then, Zuli shot up as though she had ants in her pants. She was restless but, with an authoritative voice, announced how they had promised to help Gulnar's daughters with their homework. And with that, after Lamar profusely thanked the queen and king, they bolted.

Seconds before the door shut behind them, the queen managed to fire one last question, "Will you be around tomorrow night?"

"Yes, he will be, Mother," snapped Zuli.

"Then we will be honored if you would join us for dinner. We enjoyed your company and look forward to seeing you again tomorrow. Good evening."

Zuli and Lamar sped towards the exit, this time leaving the palace through the main door. The delicious food was certainly the highlight of the evening. Leaving the palace as any regular person would, versus sneaking in like a burglar, was an added bonus. There was one other high point – the king told him that since he enjoyed literature, he was welcome to spend as much time as he wished checking out the books in the palace library. Upon hearing that statement, Zuli had broken into a wide smile and gladly reiterated her father's suggestion.

With no time to spare, they sprinted towards their one true safe haven. If anyone had been watching, they would have concluded that the two were being chased by a wild beast and that their lives were at imminent risk.

Gulnar served them ice water so they could cool off. They recounted the entire evening to her, talking over one another with much excitement, and adding more and more embellishments. They were thankful to have dodged the last question posed to Lamar by the queen.

"You'll be so proud of me, Gulnar," Zuli declared. "I told my mother we had promised to help the girls with their school project and bolted out of there."

The nanny was more worried than proud. She smiled at them, realizing how very perfect they looked sitting beside each other and how in love they were. Of course, the queen noticed the dynamism. Zuli and Lamar fooled no one but themselves. Their love had a life of its own. It was virtually palpable.

After a full night's rest in their respective sleeping arrangements, Zuli rushed out of bed to go wake Lamar so they could start upon another adventure. It was a crisp and sunny day in Kabul. The sky above was a spotless blue oasis. Zuli and Lamar had a full day to explore the city. While more modern ways of life had taken root in Kabul, Afghans still had to behave according to traditional rules in certain sections of town, and certainly outside of Kabul's parameters.

Since they were venturing in an older area of Kabul, they could neither hold hands nor be playful with each other. All they could do was walk side by side, with ample room between them and unflinchingly serious expressions. Zuli donned her mother's oversized sunglasses to thwart facial recognition from any royal fans.

When she was younger, Lamar had followed Zuli around town as her protector. He was unaware then, but during their enchanted journey to find the unseen fig blossom, he discovered that they were soulmates designed to come together and be as one. Even then, she had been most creative when she disguised her real identity. It allowed her to be free among her own people, the citizens she wholeheartedly admired. He glanced at Zuli and his entire being filled with joy. She was so beautiful, and Lamar was enamored by her inner and outer charm. *Those sunglasses were meant for her face. She looks like a movie star,* he reflected.

Regardless of the restrictions, Zuli enjoyed the outing more than when she browsed the market with Gulnar or when she used to sneak out of the palace in full disguise. Lamar took her to places she had never before visited, even passing by his home on their makeshift tour of the city. Every street vendor they made purchases from was familiar with Lamar. The vendors made each dish with care and attention, some spicy, some salty, and others sweet. Lamar and Zuli's mouths watered at the combined aromas, as they inhaled the banquet of smells. A few even prepared larger portions at no extra charge. Lamar thanked and tipped them. Some were unfamiliar with accepting an extra reward for work they considered to be their commonplace duty. But, after an exchange of niceties, they surrendered the struggle and accepted Lamar's generosity.

They shared a huge bowl of *aushak* while Lamar told her about his great-aunt's obsession with the dish. She never missed an opportunity to talk about, make, and eat the dumplings. Following lunch, they entered stores selling a myriad of Afghan rugs, traditional clothing, and lapis artifacts. In every store they visited, Zuli had to stop Lamar from spending all his money on her. She would not accept anything else especially after he had already presented her with a most exquisite and expensive ring.

"I hope you don't mind me asking, Lamar, but where did you get the money for the ring? Please tell me you didn't deplete all of your savings," Zuli said.

Lamar told her about his bank account. After she discussed the nation's impending unrest with him, he had decided to hold on to his money in case of a sudden invasion. However, he assured her that he still had enough left over to support himself for the foreseeable future.

Their last stop of the day was to meet his old friend, the flower vendor. Lamar attested that the lush bouquet she received was from this vendor. He told Zuli about how his mother had always sent him to buy flowers from Sakheegul. Lamar's family knew him for many decades. Before they had reached the other side of the river, Zuli knew Sakheegul's entire life story. Sure enough, the old man was elated by the sight of Lamar. His tired, distinguished face was etched with expressive deep lines, each clearly signifying joy, love, laughter, pain, and loss. Above all, he physically embodied the history of a nation, now a war zone, that had gone from peace and concord to unrest and disorder.

An excited Sakheegul took Zuli's hand and held it tight. "How lovely you are," he said to her. He promptly followed up by shaking Lamar's hand, as if he was congratulating him on choosing a perfect companion. He had no idea who Zuli was.

They chatted until dusk, sharing the fruits and cookies they had bought earlier that day. Sakheegul was taken aback by their unprovoked kindness. Lamar had a keen admiration for souls that embodied the wisdom and the hidden meanings of life and loss. Surely, it was in the magic of silence where the voice of inner pain was concealed. His friend safeguarded his pain all too well.

They listened to the artful and sensible words of the old, but young at heart, flower man, "This world requires you to always be soulful, colorful, wonderful, mindful, careful, and faithful. In other words, as soulmates, be in love and fully in awe of one another. Your connection by the strands of your souls shall ensure that you remain focused, always within the present moment, so that you are not led astray or misplaced. This nation is in dire need of *you* and *you*," he said, pointing to Zuli and then to Lamar.

He gestured to all of his flowers, "Please have your pick of whichever flowers you would like. Look at this tulip. It's the perfect example of a cup of love, but it also has many scars of the heart. You know, Rumi said it best, 'God writes spiritual mysteries on our heart.' I say, if you look carefully at small details, you'll see signs of such writings in nature and all around the world. I wish I had more to give you both, but I'm afraid this is all I have, a poor man's offering – a small garden of flowers."

Lamar picked a single white rose. He warmly smiled and said, "This is all we need, my friend. After all, a willing heart is a giving heart. *Wings* – This white rose reminds me of the luxurious wings of Sadaf, the mother dove, who shall never be forgotten. From The Garden of Roses, she elevated to mighty, skyscraping heights."

"Love, give me back my wings. Lift me, lift me nearer."
~ *Hafiz*

He turned to Zuli. "It was in that moment, you and I, we found ourselves at the threshold of the heavens. I meditated upon this phenomenon and thus concluded that wings were granted to the citizens of the world – we are all like Sadaf with lucent wings. In the history of existence, human minds have been the creators of our very own demise. When our bright certainties turn into dark realities, words and actions take root and roots offer its bitter fruits. That is why those who have also contemplated know all too well: we have the power to soar to realms above realms.

"Zuli, in my sorrowful times, in between my solemn prayers, my pleading words rose beyond such realms. When it felt as though a lock willfully unlocked within my chest, it was then that it became too clear – even words have wings. Genial words are the key to unlocking wishes – inimical keywords are those that forever lock us up, amidst our painful tears, to suffer and suffer more. Lucky for me, Zuli, over the years Sakheegul has always been generous with his words."

He paused with a chuckle, "Words as sweet as the perfume from the rose you've plunged your nose into!"

As dinnertime approached, they parted with Sakheegul and headed back to the palace so they had enough time to freshen up. Zuli wanted Lamar to stop by earlier to spend more time exploring the library together.

"Come to the front entrance in an hour. I will open the door for you. Dinner starts promptly at eight, so we can go to the library beforehand. I love you, my love," Zuli whispered as she hugged Lamar.

As soon as Zuli and Lamar walked from the library to the dining room and took their seats at the table, the fiery evening began.

The first question was posed to Zuli. "Have I seen that ring you're wearing? As a matter of fact, I don't ever recall seeing it before," the queen said while she kept her eye on the ring.

The king was intrigued by the question, and he, too, turned his attention from his plate to Zuli's finger. He had been so preoccupied with news of nationwide unrest that the ring was a welcome distraction.

Lamar had a most perfect bite of food piled on his spoon, ready to be enjoyed. Upon hearing such a remark, however, he shut his widened mouth and dropped his utensil onto his plate with a *clink*. He had lost his appetite.

With some luck and perfect timing, Gulnar walked in, saving Zuli from even more trouble.

"Oh, here you are," the queen said. "My dear, I was just asking Zuli about the ring on her finger. It goes so well with her pearl necklace. Have you ever seen this piece before?"

Only to Zuli and Lamar was it obvious that even Gulnar was stunned into momentary silence by that unexpected question. Two days ago, she had seen the ring on Zuli's finger, but never questioned her about it. However, it had been painfully obvious that Lamar had given it to her. After all, no matter what time of day, Zuli was transfixed by the ring and she admired it nonstop.

Gulnar spoke with a calmness that almost had Zuli and Lamar fooled.

"Your majesty, if you recall, a few weeks ago the girls and I went shopping with Princess Zuli. The princess decided to purchase this ring with her saved-up birthday funds."

The confused and surprised queen contorted her eyebrows so that they were raised much higher than their normal resting position. The king, on the other hand, was far from bothered, likening its design to that of the Crown Jewels of England.

The conversation quickly dissolved as Gulnar asked the queen whether she wanted a post-dinner drink of green tea or black coffee.

Tomorrow was a day Lamar was not looking forward to. According to what they had shared with everyone, his visit with his pretend cousin, Gulnar, was coming to an end. Indeed, the days had dwindled, but the cherished memories had taken root within his heart.

"Above all else, guard your heart, for it is the wellspring of life."
~ Proverbs 4:23

Lamar left a tearful Zuli under the trees in their secret hideaway. He kissed her tears away and promised to call on her tomorrow.

CHAPTER SIX
Liberty And Dignity

"Be still and know that I am God."
~ The Bible [Psalm 46:10]

"Here he is, I found him! Be careful, we have to remove all the debris before we pull him out," yelled a disembodied male voice.

Why can't I breathe? What happened to my voice? Lamar was in numbing pain. It felt like he was trapped between two gigantic rocks.

"No, don't touch that." Lamar heard a soft female voice. He felt an unfamiliar hand touch his arms, neck, and chest. The hand placed a foreign object over his face, covering his nose and mouth. Cool air went up his nostrils.

The sounds of morning prayers woke him up. He sat straight up and fell back down in excruciating pain. Pinching sensations crept through him, concentrating mostly in his arms. *I must wake up. This awful dream must end.*

Lamar heard an approaching pair of footsteps stop by his side. Several people conversed. Nothing they said made sense. *Who were they talking about?* He heard the same female voice from before: "Yes, doctor, he is showing signs of progress. His vitals are stable and his blood pressure is back to normal. He has regained consciousness several times and has even attempted to sit up. Should we lower the dosage of the pain medication? This is his sixth day near-comatose."

Before slipping back into unconsciousness, Lamar heard his grandfather's whisper, reminding him to pray for his heart's desires and well-being during the day, to never miss those immersive moments in the sacredness of praying at the break of dawn and brink of dusk. He always reminded him to pray for others before himself. Lamar fought the urge to drift off again and tried to finish praying.

He struggled to prop himself up by his elbows and was gently pushed back down in place. A plastic device that covered his nose and mouth was removed; it was an oxygen mask. A rush of cool air hit his face and he slowly blinked against a harsh light overhead. "If you can hear me, please tell me your name. Last week, you were brought to the hospital where you've been recovering well. Open your eyes, it's time to wake up. Don't try to sit up again because you're hooked up to many different machines. Do you understand?"

He understood everything. However, all he wanted to do was sleep. With as much effort as he could muster, he mumbled, "Lamar, Lamar..."

The female voice repeatedly echoed his name and asked him to wake up. The mental fog began to clear and he was enveloped by a sudden sensation of awakening. He opened his eyes.

"What's today's date? What time is it?"

An entire day then passed after regaining consciousness. With severe head trauma and newly stitched wounds, he was still too weak to leave. The nurse placed a firm pillow behind him and he sat up.

Laily, the nurse, was an older lady who tended to all the patients who needed intensive care. She told Lamar that he had been brought to the hospital by a bearded man who had dug him out from under a massive pile of debris. "You're a lucky young man to not have broken any bones," she said.

Lamar recounted all that he could remember to Laily. "I was at home getting ready for bed when I heard an explosion. When I looked up, my roof was gone. For just a second, I saw a sky filled with the brightest stars, but then it felt like I was being crushed by a boulder. That's all I recall."

The nurse explained, "Last week, the Russians invaded Kabul. God have mercy on our homeland! The city has come under devastating rocket attacks. Many homes and businesses have been demolished and thousands of innocent lives have been lost. An even greater number of citizens have fled the country. Military tanks are situated at every major intersection and building, including the political offices and Kabul's radio and television stations. Plus, there are many low-flying fighter jets circling the city around the clock. They're targeting anything that moves. They've already destroyed a military base, ministry buildings, and part of the royal palace."

"Where are the king and his family?" Lamar blurted out in a sudden state of panic.

"On the first night of the attacks, the palace was targeted by both air and ground forces. The king and his family have been captured, but no one knows who among them is still alive. Why do you ask, are you part of the king's family?"

Lamar choked back a horrified scream that was just about to burst out of him. His eyes, instead, flooded with tears. Pain wounded his heart, mind, and soul. To preserve the sanity of the wounded, tears were the antidote.

"I would like to be left alone now. I need some rest. Thank you for taking care of me, Ms. Laily. Stay safe," Lamar said.

The morning sun was on the verge of breaking through the barriers of the horizon. Lamar hobbled out of his room and peered into the eerily empty hallway. A closet across his room was slightly ajar. He walked to it and pushed the creaky door open. Inside, he found a pile of clothes that belonged to men, women, and children. These were the garments torn from patients who were now corpses, some known, others permanently unidentified. Since the clothes were mostly drenched in blood, the pile was likely going to be incinerated. The smell of death coupled with dried blood seemed strong enough to kill any remaining living creature.

Lamar could hardly walk, but he was not going to lie in a hospital bed when Zuli was in danger. *Of course, she is still alive*, he thought. Neither bullet, fire, rocket, nor evil would tear her away from him. If she perished that day, he, too, would have died in that rocket attack. He survived because she was still alive. They were one.

With a full bottle of painkillers in his pocket, Lamar exited the near-empty hospital onto an even more desolate street. There were very few people out and about. The morning prayers could be heard from far away. People's belongings, shoes, clothing, toys, and precious blood covered the ground. Homes were destroyed and stores had been abandoned. Collapsed walls, burned trees, and shattered glass were all that was left. Smoke hovered over Kabul, a city that had already suffered from years of civil unrest. His place of birth looked completely foreign to Lamar, a graveyard in the making.

His birthplace had been invaded. It was an invasion of human liberty and dignity. A harrowing ordeal awaited, one that terrified the prudent nation. Hell had manifested its wrath on his country.

Lamar hid behind a crumbling brick wall as a line of Russian tanks rolled by. He picked up a rock, waited, and as the last tank passed, flung it with utter disdain. It hit its target without even making the smallest dent. Lamar stood over the tracks as the tanks continued on the road. He spat and cursed, kicking the crisscrossed twisted imprints under his feet. The human mind created such a sophisticated piece of machinery that only led to self-obliteration and mass destruction. This was a holy land, a beating heart, where his parents and loved ones had been laid to rest. Now, this land was imploding from its core. The Russian leaders were globally renowned for the ruthless treatment of their own people. What atrocities were they going to commit in the poor nation of Afghanistan?

When the tanks drove through the streets and rolled over manicured grass, they narrowly missed two perfect daisies. The flowers were still rooted to the ground through a slight break in the asphalt and barely avoided getting crushed. Not a petal was askew. These beacons of hope bemused him, as these most delicate flowers were still intact while everything else had already perished.

As excruciating pain swept through his body, Lamar bent down to pluck the flowers. He pulled them from the ground and held them up against the gray sky overhead. The flowers were a sun against such a dark ether. He took it as a sign of luck and light to come. He placed both in the pocket of his shirt, over his heart.

He felt an unrelenting tug at his heartstrings. It was all too obvious: a path between their hearts still existed. Though, this path was designed to remain unseen and would only reveal itself to the seeker once the agony of separation stirred in one's depth. Undoubtedly, moons upon moons, nights and days would pass in utter agony. Surely, Zuli would guide and lead him to her by the twined fibers of their hearts.

Lamar sighed and thought, *Let the sun come out, let my Zuli appear on my path, do not let me be crushed by misery. If the sun refuses to shine, then the moon chases away the darkness. After all, Zuli wrote her first love letter under the gaze of the moon.*

Lamar arrived at his home, the shoe repair shop. It had been reduced to a mountain of dirt, collapsed walls, and tangled wires. He circled around the ruins. Most of his belongings had been burned. Luckily, he could just see the edge of his father's small desk buried under a part of the roof. His bed was partly burned, but it was still identifiable. He spent hours removing the rubble until a small passageway had been opened to retrieve whatever remained of his personal belongings.

Just then, a little boy approached him. "What are you doing?" the child inquired in a tiny frightened voice.

The boy, Sabir, was his neighbor, the bread baker's youngest son. Although timid around strangers, he agreed to crawl through the opening and get the belongings Lamar needed.

With a bag of salvaged items in hand, Lamar followed little Sabir to his home behind the bakery. The unfriendly baker from across the street who had baked his bread over the years, Najib, was the man who had saved his life. Najib recounted the entire incident to Lamar. It took him and his friends all day to dig Lamar out from under the remains of his home without injuring him further.

The baker was most caring. He had visited Lamar in the hospital twice, bringing freshly baked bread, cheese, and fruits. He left the food for the nurses and other patients while Lamar was unconscious. When he heard this, Lamar was at a loss for words. All he could do was hug Najib. The grown men cried in each other's arms. They shed tears for the loss of their motherland, as well as the loss of independence and individuality. They knew that more citizens would die and that even the death of human rights was imminent, for there was no palpable assurance of a prosperous future. Regardless of the storm ahead, Lamar hoped that eventually darkness would lead to a glimpse of daylight. After all, Afghanistan, known as the 'Graveyard of Empires,' was a self-reliant and resilient nation. Surely, they would overcome this invasion.

Najib was on the verge of taking his children and wife to Bangladesh, only to return once peace was restored. Yet again, luck had taken a sudden turn and Lamar's future had drastically changed – he knew he had to find Zuli.

Later that afternoon, Lamar decided to venture towards the palace. Najib insisted on accompanying him. As they trekked to the royal palace, Lamar told Najib that he had good friends working there who he wanted to check up on. The closer they got, the weaker Lamar felt. Smoke billowed above them. The walls had been blown to pieces and the magnificent ancient palace door had been reduced to shards of splintered wood. Lamar could make out the door frame that had remained somewhat intact. The area was guarded by a battalion of tanks. He stood back while Najib approached the Afghan soldiers to ask some questions.

"The entire royal family has been imprisoned. Apparently, the king and many of his close family members have been injured. The women, children, and elderly will be given permission to leave as soon as the international humanitarian organizations reach an agreement. Only then will the king and his remaining family members be granted asylum in an allied country."

Lamar headed back to Najib's home, completely shattered. Thanks to Sabir, he still had his new jacket with all his money intact in the inner pocket. The note where he scribbled his vows to Zuli was there, too. He had planned to ask Zuli to write her vows on the same piece of paper, so they could sign it and seal their love forevermore. He still had the magical silver-tipped tree branch to his name. He changed into his own clothes and discarded what he had on. He was going to spend the next week gathering information on the whereabouts of Zuli's family. The only speck of optimism he could hold on to was the small piece of paper and the photograph he had found while counting his money. Along with a stunning snapshot of herself, Zuli had cleverly tucked a note in his pocket as she had done on their enchanted westward journey. He tenderly touched each word and kissed the imprint of her deep scarlet lipstick she had left on the paper. He inhaled the faint smell of her lingering perfume and briefly felt her in his embrace once more.

Lamar wandered the streets surrounding the palace, reduced to a ghost of a man. The cruel hands of destiny had inflicted severe wounds upon his soul. At night, he prayed and quietly wept. Najib fed him and kept a close watch on him. Lamar became more and more depressed, drowning in the dark well of sorrow. He no longer mourned the deaths of his parents and little sister. He mourned the death of himself.

After many excruciating days without updates, an official broadcast by Radio Kabul announced that Afghan rebels targeted and have continued their attacks on the government.

"A treaty was signed with our friendly neighbor, Russia. They are our guests and have offered to assist in the fight against the rebels to establish law and order across the country. Any man, woman, or child who does not abide by the rules and regulations will be apprehended as an enemy of the land."

What the announcer did not publicize was the *truth*. The rebels were indeed fighting the current regime – one that had been established by the extremist Afghan Communist Party and was backed by the Russians. It was a totalitarian system, marked by nothing but the oppression and demoralization of human worth and sovereignty.

The broadcast continued, "It has become apparent that the king's cousin played a catastrophic hand in overthrowing the monarch. The republic form of governance did not last long before the king and his cousin faced their eventual fate."

Lamar shook his head. "Now, the outbreak of a bloody Afghan-Russian war will only act as a breeding ground for the methodical death of this nation."

Most disturbing was the very end of the radio announcement: *"We belong to God and to God we shall return."* There was a long pause. Lamar was engulfed by a numbing chill. Najib closed his eyes. They braced themselves.

"The king is dead."

Another prayer was said. The broadcast went silent.

Kabul's high school and college students organized massive walkouts to protest the invasion of their country. They chanted and threw rocks, and in return, were showered with bullets. The bodies of girls and boys were collected and thrown like worthless junk into military jeeps. Parents frantically searched for their children who were long dead and could never return home. Massive graves were dug in the dark of night. Teachers, politicians, businessmen, brothers and sisters, sons and daughters, and mothers and fathers were executed and buried. Lovers were torn apart, weddings were canceled, and funerals were attended, one after another. Identities were obliterated. Lives were demolished. Hope was bulldozed.

The great Rumi said: *Being a candle is not easy. In order to give light, one must first burn.* Kabul burned and the light it emanated was from the cries of the innocent, both of Earth and of Heaven.

Lamar remembered when he and Zuli were in the garden of roses. Within the garden, it was not the face of one rose that had shone the most. It had been the totality's scent and beauty that gave the garden life. The image of the white rose petals rising to the sky was vivid in his mind. It was then that love had conquered the evil crows. To kill the innocent and defenseless was the presence of evil and the absence of amity. How could light conquer hate within his doomed reality? The miracles of life and love, including the sun's brilliance, had been extinguished, and the rising lethal smoke choked and stifled pleas for freedom. Even the splendid words of Hafiz no longer applied: *Carry your heart through this world like a life-*

giving sun. The nation's heart was broken, and Lamar's inner light had paled.

Power-driven and selfish rulers were individuals raised, foremost, with the absence of reverence for oneself and humanity. Animosity directed their moral compasses with fatal, yet fundamental, egocentrism. The root of such animosity must be severed to set them free of all enmity.

His promise to Zuli, that he would visit her the day after their royal dinner, was broken by the hands of tyranny. Had she fought against being taken away without him? *Of course, she did,* Lamar thought. She was the queen of his aching heart and the ruler of their boundless ocean of emotion. He missed her with every beat of every breath left in him. The colors drained from dawn and dusk. Without Zuli's shining face, tender touch, and lovely smile, he no longer saw beauty. The flowers began to wither and fade, and the world shrank so small that he no longer felt like he fit – an inapt existence.

Just a glance from Zuli made him drunk. He felt like dancing about, like the leaves stirred by a breeze that traveled from the valleys of bliss. Zuli embodied charm and class, like a timeless majesty. Long ago, when she roamed the streets of Kabul in disguise to hide her regal bearing, he was her protector. As he followed her, he secretly fell for her. He vowed to find his Zuli.

A week after the first announcement, Radio Kabul broadcasted a short statement for the already sparse populace:

"Last night, with heavy security, the king was laid to rest. The grounds shall remain undisclosed. The United States of America granted asylum to the remaining family members. As fate would have it, an era of monarchy came to an absolute end. Early this morning, the royal family of Afghanistan bid farewell to this land and boarded American military aircrafts during the night. Today, they will land in Germany. Those who were injured will receive medical assistance. They will then cross the great 'Sea of Atlas,' known as the Atlantic Ocean, to start anew in America. This country will once again rise and thrive. Our leaders are dedicatedly working for the well-being of the nation..."

Najib switched the radio off and cursed under his breath. "What will you do now, my friend?"

"I will find a way to go to America. You must come with me, Najib," Lamar pleaded. "We can journey together."

Najib would soon find out from his customers that the radio broadcast had been entirely misleading. In reality, no one knew the whereabouts of the deceased king's family. This bit of news clutched Lamar tight and further pushed him into a pit of sorrow.

Lamar crossed the shaky bridge on a mission to find Sakheegul, his friend, the flower seller. Most stores were closed and just a few vendors were still operating. He learned from those who were associates of the flower man that his home had been hit in one of the nightly air attacks. Lamar set off to find the home. It had been demolished. No one could have survived such a horrific attack. A few children dug through the rubble and told him that the old man had been taken to the hospital. One of the boys said that most of his belongings had been looted by a group of teenagers.

Lamar ran back to the hospital. He asked to speak to nurse Laily, but it was her day off. A different nurse approached him, and he was met with the heart-wrenching news that his friend would no longer be selling flowers. After decades of bringing a dash of color and a touch of beauty with his array of flora by the river, the flower man had perished alone – his flowers and all the colors had vanished.

One of the nurses told Lamar that there had been no identification on the old man. He had passed the day before under her care and was going to be buried alongside the other patients who had not been claimed by family members. *Such is an unfaithful world,* Lamar thought. Arrangements were made with the hospital administration to release the body to Lamar.

With Najib's help, they buried Sakheegul in Lamar's family plot, situated by his parents. They placed whatever flowers they could find, along with bunches of green leaves, on his grave. They poured water over the dry soil, lifted their hands heavenward, and prayed for his soul to rest in utter peace. Before they returned home, they went back to Sakheegul's neighborhood and informed them about the burial so his family could visit their beloved's final resting place one last time. Yet another existence slaughtered and family left marred.

Roots had been torn up. Already, close to a million people left whatever semblance of comfort they had to avoid eventual devastation. They hoped to build new homes in neighboring countries. Afghans were housed in refugee camps along the border and were subject to horrific mandates. Lamar's plan was to avoid such an unlucky fate. Thus far, his own fate had already been tested beyond all measures.

In the entire universe, only one soul supported Lamar and ensured that he remained optimistic: *Najib*. His name befitted him, as it meant 'noble.'

The Russian army and the Afghan freedom fighters were at the edge of conflict. The most powerful army was faced with unexpected resistance from the least powerful. The Afghans used ancient weapons when fighting to liberate their country. They battled with their will. The major roads and valleys became death traps. Many who were compelled to escape by foot, vehicle, or other means were subjected to assault. Lamar was talked out of leaving the country.

"Do not rush situations like this. You must remain out of sight and carefully plan your escape." Najib stunned Lamar by quoting English novelist Edward Bulwer-Lytton, *"'The pen is mightier than the sword.'* You are a highly educated young man who could become a mentor for Afghan children.

"In this horrific warfare, both sides are looking for young males like you to join them. You have much more to offer the world that you cannot fulfill if you get killed. Stay here for as long as you want. The only flourishing businesses are bakeries. It's the only food that most can afford to purchase. I will help you in any way. You're like my own son now," Najib said.

Most of the female-only schools had already closed. Russian soldiers were known to abduct women right off the streets, a trend that horrified everyone. Parents were petrified and reluctant to send their daughters out, but their sons still had the freedom to continue their education. Lamar decided to offer free classes in Najib's home for the neighborhood girls.

Due to the constant warfare and lack of security, Najib's children left school and became both his students and classroom assistants. The number of students who wished to attend his classes pleasantly amazed him. From grades one through ten, he created a timetable with hour-long slots for each age group. Since he could not cover all the usual school subjects, he only taught what he believed was most beneficial. The one topic he taught all his pupils, without exception, was English. Even though his own grasp of the language was not entirely fluent, he was able to teach the youth the basics of such a universal tongue.

One afternoon, while class was in session, there came a knock on Najib's door. Petrified that their secret operation had been compromised, all the children were ushered into a back closet and a makeshift curtain was drawn to conceal the classroom space. Lamar slowly moved towards the door, rehearsing the phony story he would present to any suspicious agents. To his surprise, he opened the door and looked down at a mild-mannered elderly lady who appeared to be more frightened than he was. She looked as though she had overcome life's greatest hardships, but she spoke without even a hint of animosity or self-righteousness.

"Hello, Mr. A– I mean, Mr. Lamar. Please don't be alarmed. I apologize for the sudden intrusion, but I would love to be of any assistance. May I come in, if you don't mind? I'm afraid of being out on the streets and getting apprehended or – "

"Please, please," Lamar urged, as he moved aside and opened the door wider for her to step inside.

She continued, "My name is Nasira and I am a teacher. Up until the latest attacks, I was employed, but now my school is completely gone. Through some of your students, I heard about your secret tutoring program and wish to provide my help and expertise. I'm alone in this world, but I love children. I understand if you can't pay me, but I'm more than willing to work so long as food is provided for me."

Nasira glanced down at her hands, fingers fidgeting with the corner of her headscarf. "Even at this stage of my autumn years of adulthood, I'm learning that life is not a rosy journey;

it's a battle. Whether we like it or not, we will fight unexpected and unfair personal battles in addition to worldly ones. Issa's meaningful words reveal his astute observation about such strives that, '*In a world of grief and pain, flowers bloom – even then.*' The heart knows how to be the frame, love knows where to blossom, and how to paint the world with the colors of all the seasons without losing its own inner core. Must we go to the core of the pain in order to be freed? Indeed, we must. Indeed, this is what you are doing, professor."

Lamar was instantly touched by her candor and wisdom. A deal was struck, and Ms. Nasira joined Lamar in teaching the young girls.

In the evenings, after he graded papers and prepared the next day's lessons, Lamar assisted Najib as the bakery's shop clerk. The front of the bakery was dome-shaped and had windows on each wall. There was a little slot in the middle where he took the buyers' orders and money, and handed out their purchases. Najib's wife baked sweet bread, which was most popular with customers. Lamar was thankful to have a paying job, and he saved every bit of his earnings.

In three months' time, after summer and before winter, he would set off on an autumn journey to find his heart, Zuli.

§

❧ *Another Dimension* ❧

"The hidden world has its own clouds and rains, but in a different form.

Its skies and sunshine are of a different kind.

This is apparent only to a selected few who are the refined ones.

Those who cannot be deceived by the seemingly completeness of the ordinary world."

~ Rumi

§

CHAPTER SEVEN
Princess Zuli

"**P**rincess wake up! Zuli, Zuli..."

"Please stop shaking me. I'm trying to sleep," Zuli mumbled. She covered her ears and rolled over. There were so many overlapping sounds coming from outside; she did not think she would be able to fall back asleep. Something was not right. She shot up, panicked, rubbing her bleary eyes. And then, it hit.

Her loud scream was drowned out by a deafening explosion. Before she could even react, another blast rattled the palace walls, shaking both her and her bed frame. Her bedroom windows were blown out, and shards of broken glass clung to the edges of the windowpane. Her mother, nanny, and her daughters were huddled together in her room. The girls clutched each other tightly and hid behind Zuli's dresser.

"Get dressed right now," stressed the queen. "We are under attack. We only have a few minutes to leave before we are either apprehended or killed. Hurry!"

Just then, her bedroom door flew open and a dozen palace guards stormed in. "All of you must leave at once," one of them yelled.

Rapid popping sounds filled the air. Bullets penetrated the palace walls. Yes, they were under attack from all directions. While standing in the doorway, a guard was hit square in the chest. As she internally panicked, a shell-shocked Zuli ran across the room to her closet and changed her clothes. The girls had not stopped screaming and crying. They could do nothing but watch the guard profusely bleed out on the bedroom floor. The other guards stood in formation in her bedroom, shooting back from the broken windows. *What were they shooting at?* Zuli wanted to see. *Were they aiming to kill her? Had they shot the other guards on the palace grounds?*

There was no time to wonder about such matters. They had to leave. She grabbed her notebook and the pebbles she collected from when she last saw Adir. She threw open her bottom dresser drawer and fished out the ring and her grandmother's pearl necklace from her jewelry box. She dropped both in her jacket's inner pocket. She did not want her mother to see the ring on her finger or know about the necklace.

They rushed towards her parents' room. They stopped before a large bookcase in the corridor. Three guards pushed it to the side exposing the wall behind. Dust overwhelmed the air and momentarily clouded Zuli's vision. One guard bent down and lifted a single wooden plank from the floor. He reached both hands into the narrow opening and gritted his teeth. Bracing his feet against the floor, he pulled at a hidden rusted handle. An echoing crack came from behind the wall.

 The other two guards crouched down and, on the count of three, began to demolish the wall. They hit at the plaster with the butts of their rifles until a pile of pulverized dust sat at their feet and a three-foot hole had been formed in the wall. The three guards crawled in first. One of the remaining men motioned for the women to follow suit.

He explained, "This tunnel was added to the palace for a dire emergency, such as today's events. With the lever, we were able to open the otherwise impenetrable doors on either end of the tunnel. The tunnel starts off small, so you must go in single file. It widens out significantly, so before you know it, you will all be able to walk towards safety."

The air was musty. Without their flashlights, they would have been in pitch-black hollowness. As they walked down the seemingly endless expanse of darkness, Zuli grabbed her mother's arm. "Where is Father? We have to wait a bit longer. I'm not leaving without him."

"Your father is at the Ministry of Defense. He will join us soon. He wants us to leave the palace without any delay. Stop wasting time, we have to go now," her mother commanded.

Zuli trailed behind as her mother moved on, flanked by two guards on either side. She walked next to Gulnar and whispered: "I am not leaving without Lamar. I will *not*."

Gulnar replied in a hushed tone, motioning for her to keep silent. "He will find you."

The dark tunnel finally came to an end; a guard pushed open the already unlocked door. There was a scrappy old car partially obscured by large shrubbery waiting for them outside. Two other guards were in street clothes and waited by the car. They had changed out of their uniforms to not attract attention to themselves or their passengers. Further down the street, people pulled their cars over to the side of the road and either looked overhead at the jet planes or at the surrounding military tanks and jeeps. They had now been invaded by the most ruthless and heartless military force, one that was known for its crimes against civilization.

Love was the light that helped people see the ugly nature of darkness. Although that light of love had gone out in Kabul, an unbreakable innate resilience existed within every citizen. After all, man was more delicate than a flower, yet tougher than a rock. As Rumi once mused, 'What strikes the oyster shell does not damage the pearl.'

The guards in the car told the group of women that they had direct orders from the king to drive east on Nangarhar Highway. The Indian government had provided a plane for the royal family. They found out that, already, over fifty people from their family had been apprehended and imprisoned. The queen said a prayer out loud and dried her tears with a handkerchief. Even then she had a handkerchief. The queen never traveled without one. *It must have been the first thing she grabbed amid the turmoil*, Zuli thought.

"I need for this car to stop right now," Zuli yelled. "I am not leaving Kabul. I'll wait the invasion out and travel with my father. Take me to the ministry or let me out of this car." She sobbed and shouted as if being inflicted by a most brutal punishment.

"What has come over you? You will do no such thing, do you understand? You will get everyone killed. Stop yelling, you are scaring the girls. Stop it at once! We will do exactly as planned," her mother firmly stated.

Zuli already had plans; Lamar was supposed to visit tomorrow. They were going to plant flowers for Gulnar. She had a few empty flowerpots sitting on the windowsill. They were going to buy seeds and a variety of flowers from Sakheegul. They had also promised to take Gulnar's daughters to the zoo. India donated a pair of elephants and a troop of monkeys to Kabul Zoo. It was a must see.

She had been looking forward to seeing Lamar's reaction when he found her picture and love note in the hidden pocket of his jacket. Lamar told her that he kept his money in that pocket. Even though she usually looked hideous in photos, she hoped he believed otherwise. She had wanted to visit the photo shop to take a picture together. Around Kabul, there were many stores with special instant cameras used to take and develop photos for passports and other forms of identification.

Zuli had most been looking forward to talking to Lamar about writing their vows. Since the dark cloud of an invasion loomed over them, writing their commitments to cherish, trust, honor, defend, and protect one another to no known end was quite significant.

She reached a hand into her pocket. The ring was still there. With that ring they had made boundless vows of their love to one another. They declared themselves as one. Lamar's words echoed on, "Zuli dearest, under the gaze of our Creator, you are now mine and I am yours." A crushed Zuli prayed and prayed, hoping that her pierced heart would be whole once more. She felt that their love would someday pave the way to reach places where love was eternal. She knew they would find each other. Once and forever, they would raise the flag of immortal love when, finally, life would never again be lost. They would soon be holding their heads high, joyously singing the words of gratitude to the Almighty.

The queen abruptly instructed the driver to take a sudden right. She wanted to check on her sister. "We have room in this car, they will come with us. Take the backroads and don't pull up to the front of the house."

The driver was hesitant, but he dared not say a word. He did as he was told. Before long, they saw the home. It was on fire. The second story windows had been shattered and the walls no longer stood. The chaos made it difficult to see the other homes further down the road. However, it was obvious that most of the buildings had been hit, destroyed, and reduced to ashes. Afghan-Soviet troops lined the road since they knew most of the royal family lived in the neighborhood.

"May Lord have mercy on the innocent," the queen cried. They pulled into the back of her sister's home, which had remained intact. The driver slowed the car and turned off the headlights. The ladies removed their burkas. Zuli found hers unbearable to keep it on. Not only did it cover her from her head to her toes, but it also suffocated her. As a child, she wore Gulnar's burka around the palace as if it were a playtime costume. She constantly fell over herself since it was incredibly difficult to see through the mesh screen.

The guards suggested they put the burkas back on in case someone approached the car. They placed their larger weapons underneath the seats, hidden under a leather cover. They still kept their handguns under their jackets, ready to grab and shoot.

"I demand, Mother, that we leave this place at once. No one is here." Zuli called out to the driver, "Go towards the river. I'll give you directions from there. I have a friend who may need our help. Go *now*! No, Mother, I will not leave until I check on my friend," Zuli yelled through her sobs before her mother could object.

They were stopped by soldiers several times, but because they had the nightly passcode, they were permitted to drive on. They arrived at Lamar's shoe repair shop. Zuli's sobs turned into horrified screams as she broke down and wailed. She was inconsolable. Before anyone could figure out what to do with her, she climbed over Gulnar and reached for the door. She was determined to get out and see the destruction for herself. She crawled out headfirst and felt hands trying to hold her back. She kicked her feet free and fell out of the car. Her lungs filled with dust and she coughed uncontrollably. She could neither see nor breathe while wearing the burka. She took it off and ran towards the building. She screamed Lamar's name over and over again until her voice was practically gone, circling the ruins for any sign of him.

It was at that very moment that the startling and ambiguous reality of Zuli's now less-than-ideal future became apparent. Regardless of how much she tried to relate to the lives outside the palace walls, she could not shake her sheltered foundation. While she doubled over, pounding the ground with her fists, the life she imagined for herself began to crumble in an absolutely cruel and brutal nature. *All is not as it seems. All is not as it seems. All...*

Her inner voice still believed that he was alive. She had to hold on to that voice. Her intuition had never failed her before. She would not turn away from him, not now. He was all alone and may be putting himself in grave danger to find her.

The two guards lifted her from off the ground and carried her back to the car. Zuli did not resist. They drove farther and farther away from the morbid scene. Tears streamed down her face and whimpers of disbelief escaped her every few minutes. Although they could be heard by everyone in the car, no one said a word. Her mother had likely put two and two together by now.

"Gulnar, tell my mother, tell her to let me out," Zuli sobbed as she pleaded with her nanny. The car did not stop.

In the love letter she placed in Lamar's jacket, she wrote that, without him, she would cease to exist. Everything in their world had a purpose; hers was to love him. Their love was true in the purest sense of the word. Zuli knew she had been chosen for that sacred journey with Lamar. They were empowered by Adir's fundamental lessons so they could eventually contribute those principles to a greater world. They were chosen to bring joy and hope to those who felt the most pain and prejudice. They were seekers of righteousness and fairness.

It was evident that the river of virtue flowed from one source, the mountain of tragedy, to reach the ultimate ocean of hope. Humanity had one face and was crafted from one blood. Thus, all people were meant to come together to promote love and wipe out hatred. Together, Zuli and Lamar believed that trust was the only bond between the realm of hearts and souls, if untouched by the filthy hands of harm and dishonor.

In the garden of roses, they learned that the heart reflected all actions and thoughts, good or bad. During one of their heart-to-heart discussions, Lamar told her that no matter the murkiness of their realities, they must keep their hearts polished to only reflect goodness. Lamar's visions for perpetual kindness had no end. He hungered to experience life to the fullest and beamed with optimism for humanity. Regardless of all the memories, lessons, and words rushing and gushing through her, Zuli was broken. The words her father had once quoted from a long-gone Sufi seeped through the broken gaps in her heart: *All wounds and pains eventually find their way under the ground. It is there that dust and dust mesh again and souls proceed to where they belong.*

The guard in the front seat whispered something to the driver. They gave each other a nervous glance and swallowed hard. The driver asked the queen if he could share the recent news relayed to him from the Ministry of Defense. All the royal guards were outfitted with advanced communication devices, in the form of earpieces and walkie-talkies, so they could stay in contact and share updates amid the chaos. "Forgive me, your highness, but this news is jarring. His Majesty has been apprehended. Most of his ministers and generals have been..."

No more needed to be said. The guard received another message. He muttered a quick prayer to himself and lowered his head, trying to hide his emotions.

"What is it?" the queen asked.

"His Majesty has been wounded."

*To fight and conquer in all your battles is not supreme excellence;
supreme excellence consists in breaking the enemy's resistance
without fighting. ~ SunTzu*

It was all too clear now. The enemy would not cease until the land had been conquered. Only shame, not excellence, came with this oppressed ruling.

Another detour. They steered the car towards the ministry. The guards reluctantly agreed but were on high alert since the possibility of being apprehended or killed increased tenfold. Many of the soldiers assigned to protect the king were already injured or killed.

They pulled over to the side of the road. They were immediately greeted by a bright flashlight aimed at them through the windshield. Curt male voices yelled orders at them in Farsi and Russian. "Step out of the vehicle. Keep your hands up!"

A group of Afghan-Russian forces rushed towards their car, flashlights in one hand and guns in the other. The driver did what any man would do to save his own life. He switched gears, slammed his foot on the accelerator, and jolted in reverse with tires screeching. The smell of burnt rubber filled the air.

For a second, it was completely silent. The royal guards held their automatic weapons out the car windows and sprayed the oncoming soldiers with bullets. Most of them retreated, racing for cover on the open road. Some dove behind their military vehicles, crouching on the ground and returning fire. Others were struck and laid motionless in the street. By then, the driver whipped the car around and they sped off, leaving the fallen enemies far behind. They drove on unmarked streets where cars were usually not allowed to travel until he got back on the main road. They were on their way to an undisclosed location off Nangarhar Highway. Zuli's mother, the queen of Afghanistan, was on the verge of losing her homeland, throne, and life partner.

"Justice, justice thou shalt pursue." ~ The Torah

A distraught Zuli sat squished between her trembling mother and Gulnar. She did not say a word and could not muster a reaction to what had just unraveled. Emotionally, she felt every bullet that had been shot. They penetrated her heart one by one, shattering it into a million pieces. She cared not about what would happen next. In her mind's eye, she had a vision of Lamar buried under piles of wreckage. It was as though the earth she loved so much had swallowed him whole and had taken her love before she had time to love him even more. Hafiz's words persisted: *For I have learned that every heart will get what it prays for most.* It appeared that all her prayers had been buried with her heart, Lamar. She cursed the entire earth. Man should not have the ability to inflict pain on the innocent bystander for the mighty hand above us all would eventually intervene to balance the scales of injustice. Zuli, grief-stricken, mourned the process of her own slow death, as she felt her breath gradually fading. Even the moonlight was dimmer. Not one star flickered.

§

✍ *Rabindranath Tagore* ✌

"Where the mind is without fear
and the head is held high,
where knowledge is free.
Where the world has not been broken up into fragments by
narrow domestic walls.
Where words come out from the depth of truth,
where tireless striving stretches its arms toward perfection.
Where the clear stream of reason has not lost its way
into the dreary desert sand of dead habit.
Where the mind is led forward by thee
into ever widening thought and action.
In to that heaven of freedom, my father,
LET MY COUNTRY AWAKE!"

§

CHAPTER EIGHT
Uprooted

L et my country awake. Zuli wished to holler these words from the rooftops. Instead, she quietly pondered. *What could my father be feeling? Injured and defeated? He would shed a stream of tears for the fragmented country he left in fear. Now, the nation is being led towards the edge of a bottomless well of doom.*

The soldier driving their escape vehicle exited off the main highway. They were now far from civilization. Their surroundings were as barren as the Sahara Desert, with the exception of camels and caravans. Zuli could only imagine a meandering caravan of camels in tow, in perfect unison on their blurry path ahead. They would be carrying lovers over the golden sands, leading nowhere nearby, towards a far, far away paradise as a refuge from such dark nights. They would stop by an oasis where colorful tents and palm trees stood. Music would be playing, a passionate dance would last all night, poignantly circling around a warm bonfire like grains of sand, well into the morning delight.

Hitting her head on the seat, she blinked twice and shook herself out of her dazed alternate reality. The bumpy car ride on the rolling stretch of dirt and gravel turned most treacherous. They were violently rocked back and forth and thrown from side to side, to the right and the left. The car leaned forward as they rolled over a ditch. Zuli held her breath and waited for the car to tip over and fall straight into the earth. Instead, they crept onward, parking hours later with a jolt. Zuli squinted and tried to make out the dark, winged shadow ahead.

It was an Indian airplane.

The only light came from an inundation of flashlights beaming into the car's dirty windows. Large, burly men rushed towards the car, firmly clutching their loaded machine guns. As the queen emerged from out of the vehicle, they all gave a polite bow. A man in a distinguished military uniform stepped forward and quietly introduced himself to the queen. Zuli could not make out what he said, but she could tell from his pronunciation that he was not from Afghanistan. Without hesitation, they were ushered towards the plane. Flashlights illuminated their steps, so the royal family and their entourage could quickly and safely board the aircraft. A figure, presumably a crew member, stood by the plane's entrance ready to greet the group and guide them to their seats.

The queen took her first step towards the plane. She was hesitant, but, with a sorrowful deep breath, she placed her right foot on the very first step and made her way up. Zuli stepped out of line and motioned for Gulnar to go ahead of her. Gulnar's daughters clambered up and rushed into the aircraft. Gulnar lowered her head, put a hand on either railing to steady herself, and made the ascent.

Zuli could not move. She dropped to her knees, placed both hands on the dirt, and lowered her forehead to the ground. She sobbed and kissed the earth, bidding goodbye to the land she loved so dear. Her mother called out to her, urging her to hurry up.

Zuli felt like she was having an out of body experience. Surreal voices floated around her. She could envision a desperate Lamar aimlessly wandering around the empty palace grounds as though he had lost both his heart and mind. Zuli's emotions ripped through her.

Strong hands hoisted her off the ground. The soldiers picked Zuli up by her shoulders and dragged her to the plane's entrance. She had practically gone limp and struggled to regain her footing as her feet dragged and caught each cold metal step. Upon entering the plane, she clung to the steel arched doorframe as she was inundated by the sounds of mournful wails. Zuli had the dawning recognition that they were all her family members. They reached out and tried to hug the queen. Zuli still clutched her burka.

This was too much to bear. *"Bismillah, in the name of God,"* she recited under her breath. Amid the chaos, Zuli abruptly turned on her heels and darted back out of the plane. Without hesitation or considering that she could fall and break her neck, she dashed down the aircraft's stairs. When she was nearly halfway to the ground, she leapt forward and jumped off the steps. Voices echoed around her: "Zuli. Oh, Dear Lord..."

The chase was short-lived. Zuli blindly sprinted ahead. A group of soldiers pursued her. She hurtled on. Even when she could not hear them yelling for her to stop anymore, she kept running until she was forced to stop.

Zuli had lost track of time. She winced and tried to reposition herself. She was stuck in an uncomfortable crumple, her legs awkwardly tucked underneath her. She struggled to stand, even though it was no use. Zuli had fled like a wild animal escaping its hunters, before she stumbled and fell into a deep, narrow hole.

She figured that the plane must have taken off with little delay. It was too dangerous to keep it grounded to search for the princess while all the passengers' lives were at risk. Engulfed by petrifying darkness, she could not find a way out of the deep pit. She was too tired for extreme physical exertion, anyway. She had to stay put until sunrise. She leaned against the hard dirt wall and dozed off.

Later, Zuli opened her eyes, welling up with tears as she squinted against the morning rays. She could hear voices, followed by a chorus of bleating sheep. She had a plan. The simple outfit she wore underneath the burka, a beige pair of pants and oversized jacket, worked perfectly. She tore off a long piece of fabric from the burka's frayed edge and wrapped it like a turban around her head, securing her hair tightly in place. She took the tail end of the burka and wrapped it around her chest so it appeared completely flat. A short fabric scrap helped secure her throbbing ankle. Zuli concluded that the sprain took place either when she unknowingly tumbled into the hole or when she jumped off the aircraft's steps. She pulled her socks up and uncuffed her pants so they fell below her ankles. Female voices drew nearer, as did the distinct odor of sheep and goats. It was time for Zuli to think. She practiced her formulated story and worked on a newly deepened voice.

She realized that she could not easily climb out of this ditch. Although she had not been captured and forced to board the Indian airplane, she was indefinitely trapped. It was only a matter of time before vultures began to circle overhead. A shiver went down her spine. *What a horrifying feast I would make,* she thought. If she had not hurt her ankle, she would have already climbed to freedom.

Zuli noticed a small tree root sticking out of the earthy wall. She dug the front of her boot deep into the muddy soil, trying to gain leverage. As she pulled herself up, she tried to dig her injured foot in for added support. Zuli was overcome with pain and lost her footing, falling backwards with a resounding thump. She landed in a pile of her own twisted limbs. Through her injury, she let out a deep sigh and cursed loudly.

"Nana, look. Come here, there's someone trapped..." The child's voice grew near then far, presumably running back and forth between Nana and the deep pit. A female voice called out to the little boy, scolding him for straying too far. Their voices were drowned out by excited yips and howls. Zuli looked up and was greeted by a wet dog snout peering over the edge of the hole. The speckled brown canine panted excitedly, tongue out, before rounding the circle's edge.

"Malta, no," the female voice called out. Malta let out a low whine and retreated from Zuli's sight.

Zuli called out to the strangers but got no answer. Although they never acknowledged her, she could hear them having an intense discussion. When their chattering ceased, there was a light *thud,* and a rope slithered down the side of the hole. It had been knotted to a tree up above and had incremental loops knotted in so Zuli could secure her footing. She slowly climbed up, making sure not to put too much pressure on her injured ankle.

Once she neared the top, she put both hands on solid ground and began to lift herself up. The hyper Malta leapt forward and began licking her face. Zuli lifted a hand to shield herself before realizing she was losing her balance. She began to fall backwards before her saviors jumped into action. The mystery woman lunged forward and grabbed Zuli's wrist, hoisting her up until she was sprawled on the dewy grass. The little boy pulled Malta back, wrapping his arms around his neck like a makeshift leash and petting him to calm down.

"Clouds come floating into my life, no longer to carry rain or usher storm, but to add color to my sunset sky."
~ Rabindranath Tagore

What a sight to behold: a cyan expansion mingled with the nomads' vibrant, beaded dresses. Each dress was affixed with small circular mirrors and covered in hand-sewn patterns, finished with detailed oversized cuffs. As they walked, the morning light bounced off the tiny mirrors and reflected in a multitude of shimmering rays. The women wore bright scarves to cover their heads and had countless neon bangles on each hand. They had ancient gold and brass hair accessories, finished with colored gemstones. Around practically every finger were numerous oversized rings.

The nomads were known for making up a majority of the nation's poverty. They led a migratory life, herding caravans of animals. Nomads never quite integrated with society. They usually abstained from politics and other communal matters. In more recent years, per the new constitution, they were given parliamentary seats.

In summertime, whenever Zuli's family vacationed in different parts of the country, they often drove past caravans of nomads. Her father had told her how they never settled in one place and were always on the move.

Zuli recalled the king of the land wistfully muse, "What a freeing life they must lead." On occasion, her father parked the car and explored his new surroundings. He enjoyed spending time with people who lived far from the major cities. He never refused a cup of tea, a piece of bread, or a chance to chat with farmers, shopkeepers, shepherds...

Her intimidating savior spoke up, "Do you have a death wish? What are you doing in that hole? What's your name?"

The shredded burka no longer covered Zuli's face. She deepened her voice as much as she could before she replied, "My name is Z–" She stopped herself. "I fell in last night. There was an attack on our home, and I was the only member of my family to escape. I'm still not sure of their current whereabouts. They call me Zamon."

"One way or another, we're all sacrificing our loved ones to this senseless war. I'm sure your family is safe and that they will find you soon. My heart goes out to you. You're just a boy. You must be no older than fifteen, is that not so?" the tall strong female said. Zuli studied her ravishing features, from her norm-defying unibrow to her sunburnt olive skin, bearing all of life's previous hardships.

"That is so."

"They call me Safa," she told Zuli. "We're headed to Kabul to sell a few of our goats. We need the money to leave the country before we're either killed or die of starvation."

"I may not be able to walk at your pace with my injured ankle, but I need to get to Kabul too. I have a friend who may be willing to help me find my family. At this point, I have no one else in this world. I fear that, being so young, I may be recruited either by the freedom fighters or the bloodsucking invaders. May I join you on your journey? I'm guessing that it shouldn't take more than three days. Regardless, I would be happy to teach your son anything you may want."

"I know how to write my name. And I know the alphabet. And I know how to count to one hundred. And I know how to count from one hundred backwards," quipped the little boy, Jalil, gleefully.

The journey did not take a mere three days. They were often forced to hide during the day and travel at night. All the while, Zuli felt like she was a real part of Safa's family. Jalil grew close to her through his intense hunger for education. He was intelligent for his age and could have a prosperous future with access to educational resources. For now, he remained an aimless wanderer.

Malta had also taken a liking to Zuli. When he was not herding the animals, he would trot in between Zuli and Jalil, rubbing up against their legs and weaving through the grass. When they slept, Malta laid perpendicular between the two, so that his head was beside Zuli's shoulder and his tail laid on Jalil's face.

Zuli knew she wanted to adopt a dog with Lamar. Pets had not been allowed in the palace. Yet, she had immense adoration and respect for such a loyal and hardworking animal. Malta was more affectionate than most people she had met.

Her father once shared that in the western world, domestic animals were cared for as though part of a human's family. He used to quote Mahatma Gandhi, the great, non-violent leader, who led the movement for India's independence from British rule. Gandhi had acutely observed that, 'The greatness of a nation and its moral progress can be judged by the way its animals are treated.' But even a progressive mind like Gandhi's came to its own mortal limits with his cold-blooded assassination.

After a nine-day journey, they arrived. Kabul was in absolute disarray. Nothing felt familiar. The atmosphere was unwelcoming and foreign. Zuli had to cover most of her face to protect her identity. She would not be returning to the palace. She buried her former life the night she visited Lamar's collapsed home. Frankly, she never really felt at ease with the extravagant lifestyle she had been born into. Her new goal was to tend to her healing ankle and to find Lamar.

Safa's family managed to sell their goats and some of their sheep's wool for a perfectly livable profit. From the goodness of their hearts, they offered some of the money to Zuli. After they admitted her to the hospital, it came time to part ways. Jalil and Malta both found it difficult to say goodbye to Zuli. Tears were shed. Prayers were said. Their paths were forever separated.

Zuli hobbled across the hospital lobby and stood before the front desk. As she leaned against the table, an amiable, yet weary nurse approached her.

This fractured ankle is going to be such a hindrance for me, Zuli thought. Before she knew it, the nurse had begun to engage her in an uplifting conversation.

"My dear, you must rest. Don't stand on your ankle. We're going to need to hook you up to an IV because you're severely dehydrated. My name is Laily and I will take care of you."

Before Zuli could say thank you, the nurse carried on, "Until you're reunited with your family, or they come for you first, you can stay with me in my humble abode. I have provided shelter for most of my patients during these trying times."

She paused for a moment and curiously tapped her chin with a finger. "There's something unique about you. You have such a blissful aura. I sense that you're gifted in most unusual ways with a sincerely sanctified soul. Since I spend all day working with people, I like to believe that I'm now an expert on deciphering the quality of individuals' spiritual energy. I'm trying to say you appear very familiar, as if I've known or seen you before. Oh, listen to me ramble on. My words are all over the place."

Laily looked around, led Zuli into a hallway, and lowered her voice, "You deserve utmost credit to think of disguising yourself as a boy, my dear. No one is safe anymore. As a beautiful, homeless young girl, you must protect yourself. When you go out in public, I suggest you still disguise yourself. Girls have been kidnapped. Now, even young boys are being abducted. Of course, you still have the option of wearing a burka. Just know that you are always safe in this hospital."

Nurse Laily's confidence and comforting wisdom reminded Zuli of Gulnar. She, too, had an innate gift in seeing right through people. Zuli had been swallowing her physical pain and hiding her emotional wounds. She craved closeness. Before she could object, Zuli opened her arms and warmly wrapped Laily in a tight embrace. Zuli thanked her wholeheartedly for her kindness. "I don't think I could ever repay you. You're such an inspiring mother figure to me now."

Zuli held onto Laily's hand and attempted to kiss it. Instead, Laily retracted her hand and gave Zuli an even more affectionate hug. She urged her to stay strong and not succumb to despair during the dark times. "Keep your mind on your future goals and reach out with an unfurled helping hand. No incursion can dim the sun, fracture the moon, or cease creation. Even though it feels like sorrow and death are always lingering, nothing ever truly perishes. As designed, *all* is entirely renewed."

Laily released Zuli and slowly turned away. "I must go tend to other patients now. I will let you rest. Should you wish, I can talk to the head nurse about offering you a position at this hospital. We're severely understaffed and could use people like you to assist the nurses. Think it over, my dear. The doctor will be coming soon to examine you."

Zuli laid back in her cot and admiringly watched Laily disappear down the hallway. She had walked straight into the arms of an angel named nurse Laily. She was beyond lucky. She thought, again, of Lamar. She hoped he would enter her dreams and reveal his whereabouts.

Before dozing off, she recalled that seemingly harmless evening when her father had discussed the lurking unrest. How could she have known that the imminent invasion would occur practically overnight? She would have not let Lamar out of her sight. She would have stopped him from leaving the palace and made the guest bedroom his permanent home. She would have broken all the rules. Regardless of her array of options, he still slipped right through her fingers, out of reach. Who could one blame but the leaders?

Zuli gave a fake surname when she was first admitted to the hospital, yet she still dared not ask Laily about the whereabouts of the royal family. Not yet. As Lamar would say, tomorrow was another day, after all.

After a restful week, she was ready to limp around the corridors and help the nurses, patients, or anyone who needed her assistance. She had finally been hired for her first job. Her new occupation was most fulfilling and gave her a real sense of accomplishment. There was nothing more sacred than aiding the sick and caring for those on the brink of death.

Her first month on the job was the most trying and jarring. She had never witnessed so many innocent individuals in dire distress. Seeing the extent of the trauma inflicted by humans onto one another chilled Zuli to her core. Dismembered, bloody bodies never warranted an emotional reaction from killers. Their psyche was left undisturbed. Such disregard for life, alone, was enough to shake Zuli's strong foundation and destroy her already minimal trust in humanity.

Zuli never thought about medical professionals before. Why would she? She neither got sick nor ever visited a hospital. If anyone in her family came down with any illness, the doctors were promptly summoned to the palace. A few times, her mother had nurses caring for her around the clock. Now, Zuli understood that doctors and nurses were angels on earth. They chose to serve their fellow humans. They were tasked to save the weak, deliver new life, and, at times, bear devastating news. For doctors, death was only an option when all known possibilities had not been enough to save a life. Zuli could see those who had to face the dread of losing a patient were deeply disconcerted.

Laily had control of the weekly schedule and made sure she and Zuli worked the same shifts. Out of all the nurses, Laily was definitely the most talkative. Whether at work or at home, she bounced from subject to subject to pass the time. It was likely her way of keeping the pain of her daily experiences at bay. She often recanted stories her patients had told her or gave her opinion on current events. Zuli always listened politely, but never pressed her for gruesome details.

One morning, Laily brought up the royal family. "You know, I will never forget the day that Radio Kabul announced the king's passing."

Laily sighed and shuffled through a stack of medical reports before continuing. "Everyone in the hospital, from doctors to patients, shed tears and mourned his untimely fate. Since his resting place was never disclosed, everyone who wasn't working the day shift came to my house for a prayer session. It's still not clear as to where his remaining family members are. There are rumors circulating that they were transported to America, but some believe the queen and her relatives are now in India. What do you think, Zuli? We can only call upon God to keep the rest of his family safe and return them soon to this land. Zuli, are you okay? What's wrong? What's happened?"

Zuli left the questions unanswered. She bolted down the hallway – she just had to get away. She yanked one of the burkas from the nurses' station and slipped out of the emergency exit. Laily was unable to catch up with her.

Zuli was now fatherless, motherless, homeless, and hopeless.

"What is the life of this world but play and amusement? But best
is the home in the hereafter, for those who are righteous.
Will ye not then understand?"
~ Surah Al-An'am [6:32]

She headed towards the Kabul River, determined to find Sakheegul. Surely, he would know of Lamar's whereabouts. Zuli was not going to give into defeat. She had to remain strong until she reunited with Lamar.

Since it was mid-afternoon and lunchtime, the crowd was larger than usual. The street vendors were all out, trying to sustain a livable wage. She calmly made her way to where the flower vendor once greeted her ever so warmly. Yet, his stand was not there. Neither was he.

Zuli paced the adjacent streets. She entertained the idea that Sakheegul moved his operation to a more densely populated part of town. However, she asked a string of vendors the same query and was given the same regrettable news each time. She was not going to find him here.

As Zuli skulked back to the hospital, she was inundated by the tears flowing down her face. Behind the burka, she could easily conceal her sobs. She was certain that Laily would be relieved to see her again after her abrupt hospital departure.

Over the next week, a solemn Zuli committed herself to silence. She only ever spoke when she had to communicate with patients beyond a nod or shake of the head. In the evenings, back at Laily's home, she was even more stoic. Every night, she sat on the prayer rug and prayed for her dead father. Laily's instinct was to comfort her but respected her space during her silence and prayers.

Her father, the king of a land that no longer belonged to anyone, had passed away. *No, he was murdered,* she reminded herself. It pained her to think that no one from the king's family stood over his grave during the burial to pray for his soul. At the time of death, all human beings faced the same fate, which was, in turn, dependent on one's righteous or evil deeds. For the time being, her father, the son of kings, laid somewhere within the land like any other countryman before him. The earth cared not for status, title, or wealth. Dust would receive and cover a king or beggar, friend or foe, giver or taker: it mattered not. In the end, in the unseen realm, one's intentions set people apart.

❧ *Gone to the Unseen* ❧

~ Rumi

"At last you have departed and gone to the Unseen.
What marvelous route did you take from this world?

Beating your wings and feathers,
you broke free from this cage.
Rising up to the sky
you attained the world of the soul.
You were a prized falcon trapped by an Old Woman.
Then you heard the drummer's call
and flew beyond space and time.

As a lovesick nightingale, you flew among the owls.
Then came the scent of the rose garden
and you flew off to meet the Rose.

The wine of this fleeting world
caused your head to ache.
Finally you joined the tavern of Eternity.
Like an arrow, you sped from the bow
and went straight for the bull's eye of bliss.

This phantom world gave you false signs
But you turned from the illusion
and journeyed to the land of truth.

You are now the Sun -
what need have you for a crown?
You have vanished from this world -
what need have you to tie your robe?

I've heard that you can barely see your soul.
But why look at all? -
yours is now the Soul of Souls!

O heart, what a wonderful bird you are.
Seeking divine heights,
Flapping your wings,
you smashed the pointed spears of your enemy.

The flowers flee from Autumn, but not you -
You are the fearless rose
that grows amidst the freezing wind.

Pouring down like the rain of heaven
you fell upon the rooftop of this world.
Then you ran in every direction
and escaped through the drain spout . . .

Now the words are over
and the pain they bring is gone.
Now you have gone to rest
in the arms of the Beloved."

§

Zuli longed for the transitory moments, sitting under the fig tree, when she was blessed by words that journeyed from her vivid mind to be woven within her soul. She always jotted them down in her notebook, fearful of the wind blowing each here and there, scattering them all through the garden, getting tangled in the tree branches, or vanishing without a trace far beyond the clouds.

The heart is a poet when souls are apart, mused Zuli, as she scribbled word after word, page after page: *When the one who is simply one with the Beloved – it is then that time slows down. It is when the sun is elevated, brightest. The moon is dignified in your sight. The ground sits higher. Vastly glorified is the sky. Lovers lovingly loving in sight. Music beats like the pulses of their aching hearts. Only lovers dance, feet pounding upon the moving earth. The world is theirs, indeed. A blur is the past. Moments purified. Suffering rectified. Future refined. Simply as one, drunken lovers in sight. Mirrored souls, they are. Once a beautiful heart, O' ever beautiful, a lovely heart. Guard it. Nourish it. Feel it. Seal it. Forgive with it. Release it. Fragmented pieces to make peace with. Merrily, be one with the One. Merely one path exists to the One.*

"Dear God, it's me, Zuli. I'm the former princess of Afghanistan. I hope You can hear me. You took away everything from me. I have no quarrels with You, but I need to know. Did I do anything to upset You? I was chosen to travel through the most heavenly gardens so I could learn and evolve. I have acquired so much and have been continually searching for new learning endeavors. Lamar and I were chosen as peacemakers. We were ready to fulfill this honorable duty to the best of our abilities. But, look at what has taken place, setting us back a thousand years. This nation, we love. Kindly keep my mother, Gulnar, her daughters, and the rest of my family safe and sound. Protect this land, forgive the wrongdoers, and guide them back to civility. Above all, bless my father. He is with You, in Heaven, I know. After all, You are all-knowing, seeing, giving, and forgiving. Please forgive my mistakes. Shed Your mighty light and lead me on the path to Lamar; he is Your most humble believer. Show me the way with as much clarity as the darkest nights have been peppered with shining stars. Thus far, these are the darkest times of my life. I believe in You. I believe You *will* make the guiding stars shine ever so bright, and that they *shall* take the lead so I can find what I have lost. Dearest God, I pray that You have heard me. Show me a sign..."

"So I say to you, Ask and it will be given to you; search, and you will find; knock, and the door will be opened for you."
~ The Bible ~ Luke [11:9]

Following her time of reflection, Zuli broke her silence. The entire hospital staff breathed a sigh of relief. She explained to them that an old friend had been killed by the rocket attacks that had taken place weeks before. She also admitted that she missed her family dearly and was panicked because she still had no confirmation of their whereabouts. Her fellow workers hugged and reassured her that she would eventually reunite with her family. Zuli was grateful for the support but was not certain if they themselves believed what they tried to convince her of. However, it mattered not because *they* had become her family.

That evening, Laily and Zuli ate an assortment of sweets they had purchased from a shop by the hospital and sipped piping-hot green tea. Zuli piled her plate up with heaps of *jelabi,* one of her all-time favorite desserts. The fried dessert was usually pretzel-shaped and was thoroughly soaked in thick, sweet syrup. Each piece stuck to Zuli's fingers as she chowed down on the sugary treat.

Laily sat shoulder to shoulder with Zuli and cautiously brought up her recently deceased friend.

"I know his death has profoundly upset you, my dear. Of course, such news is beyond disheartening. You're still very young, but as you gather life experiences, you will understand that it's normal to share your pain with others. Yes, even sorrow is meant to be shared. That is the only way grief can be digested, processed, and understood. Alas, when the timing is right, that sadness must be released and replaced with joy to, once again, gladden the soul."

"The day I ran out of the hospital, I was also overcome with emotion for the king and his family. This beautiful land has been crushed by the iron hands of the killers of humanity. After I ran out, I wanted to get some fresh air. Before I knew it, I had already reached the shaky bridge. You know I'm a fast walker," Zuli said.

Zuli grinned and looked to Laily for confirmation. With a nod, she confirmed that very truth. At times, during their morning walk to work, Laily struggled to keep up with her.

Zuli continued, "Well, I decided to look for a friend, one I had met through another very, very good friend of mine. His name was Sakheegul, and he was known as the flower man. His flower stand was small, but it was as colorful as an entire garden of tulips, lilies, and roses. He brought a certain vibrancy to every life. Anyway, I couldn't locate him, and I discovered that he had passed on. To make matters worse, I couldn't find any details about his final days from anyone. If he had still been there, I would've brought back the loveliest bouquet of flowers for everyone at the hospital."

Laily jumped in, "I know this flower man – well, let me rephrase. I never met him, but my fellow nurses tended to him when I was off duty. They told me how he had touched their hearts with his floral vocabulary and unwavering smile up until the very moment he passed. Honestly, my dear, I could be rambling on about somebody entirely different, but this gracious man managed to charm every on-duty nurse during his last few hours on earth. He had most definitely asked the staff to refer to him as the flower man."

She poured herself another glass of tea and resumed without pausing. "If I remember correctly, the hospital released his body for burial. Two men, one young and one somewhat older, showed up to fill out the mandatory paperwork. Oh, I wonder what has become of that young man. He was one my patients, you know. That is, until he fled. When he came back to take the flower man away for burial, he originally asked for my assistance, but I was off at the time. He even left me a note apologizing for his sudden departure from the hospital while I was still tending to him. Anyway, I was told, though, that he went out of his way to reiterate to the other nurses just how close the two were."

Zuli slammed her cup of tea on the table and leapt to her feet. Laily ignored her and began clearing the table. "My goodness, Zuli, be careful! That tea is still scorching hot. Don't burn yourself."

Zuli was frantic and enlivened by a newfound vigor. She grabbed Laily by the shoulders and spun her, so they were face to face, staring at each other with widened, surprised eyes.

Zuli was practically screaming, "What, who came to the hospital? Who claimed the old man? Tell me! Who?"

"I told you, I wasn't there. Like I said, the staff told me about the return of my former patient after the fact. He was the one the nurses swooned over for his charm, good looks, and poetic expertise. He was quite well-mannered, and even recited a poem for each nurse who cared for him."

Zuli sat back down, held her head in her hands, and said, "His name was Lamar, right?"

As Laily sat back down, Zuli sprang from her seat again and yelled, "It *was* Lamar, tell me, *please.*"

Laily thumbed through a stack of personal documents and files she had brought home from work. She pulled a thin packet from the stacks, marked only by the letter *L.*

That patient was, in fact, Lamar.

§

"The Sun travels to an appointed place. This is the decree of the Mighty, the All-Knowing."

~ The Qur'an
~ Surah Ya-Sin [36:38]

§

CHAPTER NINE
The Harsh Realities

"The very center of your heart is where life begins – the most beautiful place on earth." ~ Rumi

T he birds sang their hail and ushered in the arrival of a new day. Zuli and Laily talked throughout the whole night. The two ladies barely had time to freshen up, grab a quick bite of breakfast, and arrive at the hospital for their morning shift.

The previous night, as soon as Laily confirmed Lamar's name, Zuli left the room in an exhilarated frenzy. She entered the foyer and reached into her jacket pocket. She returned to the living room, extended her hand to Laily, and held her engagement ring. "Lamar is my fiancé. He placed this ring on my finger mere days before we were separated."

Dazed by such an unexpected turn of events, Laily stuttered, "I have never seen such a unique ring before." Staring at the piece in adoration, she was stunned beyond words.

Zuli shared their love story, and Laily listened. Zuli wept, and Laily consoled her. Laily cried, and Zuli apologized for upsetting her.

"Never apologize for speaking of love and touching the listener's heart."

"You know, he kept our engagement a surprise from me. Oh, Laily, Lamar loves me very much. He purchased this exquisite piece all on his own. When he got on his knee, he told me that I was his and he was mine. I was so taken aback and nervous that, at first, I extended my right hand to him. But, as a lefty,

I should've known better. Isn't it just the most elegant ring, Laily. It's so..." Zuli trailed off, lost in admiration for her ring, as though it was her first time ever laying eyes on it.

"My love with Lamar is transcendent, just like a fanciful fable," Zuli mused. "Anything so olden is nothing less than golden. What I mean is that, through many lifetimes, our souls' fibers have been weaved and intertwined with such a complexity that no one could ever untie them. It's the kind of love, I'm sure, you've read about in love stories, like in the tale of Layla and Majnun. You two have such a similar name, too."

Zuli began to explain, "Not many know this, but his real name was Qays. People called him Majnun because he lost his mind and some thought of him as *insane*. He and Layla fell in love when they were kids. Once they grew up, they wanted to wed, but Layla's father forbade it. Instead, he married her off to a rich man. Because of this, Qays lost his mind and has now gone down in history as Majnun. There are many variations to this story, but this is the version I like the most. After his family gives up on him, Majnun spends his days wandering the desert and writing poems in the sand, hoping the wind would carry his words to wherever she was. Apparently, Layla died of heartbreak, and a dead Majnun was eventually found beside her grave."

Zuli cleared her throat, "Let me remember. Right, I believe this is the poem Majnun wrote before dying of a broken heart:

> 'I pass by these walls, the walls of Layla
> And I kiss this wall and that wall
> It's not Love of the walls that has enraptured my heart
> But of the One who dwells within them.'"

Laily dried her tear-stained face with a corner of her headscarf. "How could I not cry, knowing that such precious words arose from the shattered pieces of a heart in mourning?"

Shaking her head, Zuli continued, "Too many great loves have ended in tragedy. Has anyone ever thought of how to bypass the catastrophic side of things? The answer is simple – wretched, dark souls with malicious intentions of poisoning all pure things have to be removed from the equation so passion and affection can justly mend and restore."

"Laily, do you think that my fate and Lamar's is going to be the same as Majnun's?" Zuli queried, "Or maybe we'll end up like Farhad and Shirin. I mean, their love story was even *more* traumatic. Lamar and I would die without each other. He told me himself that without me, he would cease to exist. I clearly remember the pain of the first night after he went back home. The next day he told me that when we were apart during those few hours, that he felt torn from my essence. And he said that in the absence of my moonlight, darkness covered his entire space. Such was, obviously, true for me when I was away from him. Without sounding too wistful, in my view the ether's entire luminosity darkened. I told Lamar that he would always be the sun and I the moon. We vowed to honor this sacred relationship chosen for us by the might of the Mighty."

"You speak like an old soul, Zuli."

"I've been told. I often think I am an old soul."

Laily refrained from telling Zuli about how life's harsh realities would likely follow them like dark shadows and instead chose to paint a more uplifting image of the reality ahead.

Laily took Zuli's hand in hers, "My dear, your fate was predetermined. Look where you are now. On top of that, I was chosen to care for Lamar when he was brought to the hospital, too. It is all by design."

Zuli gave Laily a hug and lovingly placed her head on Laily's shoulder. "You would be happy to know that Lamar is even more soulful. We spent long hours discussing spiritual and philosophical ideas. We put on our analytical hats and tried to outdo each other. It's most fulfilling to be intellectually compatible, don't you agree?"

Laily gave her a slight nod of concurrence topped with a warm smile.

Zuli continued, "To be able to see and recognize the grandness of this wonderful existence with all of its wonders and endless beauties, depends on the quality of the inner eye. This seeing is granted only to those who are rooted in the spring of life with keen and clear inner vision. Hence, when the inner eye graciously sees, seeks quality, and practices rightness, light, like rays of the sun, erupts within. It cures the darkness trapped within the chambers of our hearts, so our souls can evolve and rise high. This is our Creator's wish for us. Whether we wish the best for ourselves is another matter altogether.

"Are you tired, Laily? I certainly have been told that I talk too much."

"I will never get tired of such smarts. Continue, my dear."

"I have never shared this with anyone, Laily. I was always in search of something to fill the emptiness from within. It was a looming dark night when the touch of a strong hand shook and woke me – distress was my being, despair was my foreseeing. That night, there came into my sight a superior golden light. Oh Laily, you cannot fathom how striking it was. It was delicate and refined, like a gleaming sunray. No words can define it. Indeed, this light was brilliant and vivid. I had but one choice: to revel within its rays. If you will, it was some sort of pure gilded confetti. There were yellow stars and golden dust, shimmering in perfect unison."

Laily was deeply moved by Zuli's dream. "My dear, hold on to your sacred experience. From my readings, I learned there is a special night that, from within its darkness, is a bringer of light and guidance, yet only to certain blessed souls. All I can tell you is to keep your foresight on the light. Lamar and you will be forever immersed within these sunrays to brighten paths unseen."

"Reason is a light that God has kindled in the soul."
~ Aristotle

Both ladies dozed off for a short while before the sonorous recitation of prayers woke them.

"Here, look at this love letter Lamar wrote in my notebook. I'll read just this part of it to you." Zuli carefully turned the pages until she found the letter Lamar wrote in the garden of lily ponds, under the lemon trees. She stumbled on the letter when they were traveling by carriage and Mr. Matek stopped for a night's rest. While Lamar slept under the looming willow trees, she read and reread the letter, each word lit by the moon's gaze.

"*A few years ago, when I was just a little boy, you appeared on the canvas of my mind as a new draft of the face I had seen before in the mirror of my soul. This was way, way back in time, when I was in the garden where our fig tree stands, resilient and strong. Then and there, I knew that you were the one. After all, you are noor (light). Ask yourself, what would the sun be without its radiating glints of light? It would be nothing but a dark orb. It is only I who can clearly marvel at your shine while you remain unaware of your effects upon my world. Now I see beauty at dawn and dusk, and experience joy and love everywhere in between.*"

Laily sighed, "There are no words to express my admiration for the two of you. Indeed, you *are* one."

"That was the night I realized I had fallen in love with Lamar. So now you know why I cannot, will not, rest. My fiancé is missing, but I know he's alive. I can feel it. I know he's desperately searching for me. I'll find my Lamar, even if it takes me the rest of my life."

"Where is the fig tree he mentioned in his letter? I love figs."

"We have a special... magical, if you will, fig tree in the garden of Ali Mardan. Without knowing it, we both used to visit the same tree when we were children. Have you visited the garden?"

"Yes, it's one of my favorite spots. I used to go there with my school friends. We picnicked many times under that same fig tree. There was always this certain calm, a welcoming kind of effect that I sensed whenever I visited this particular park."

"Oh, Laily, I hope that we can visit it again soon. Maybe, someday, I'll tell you this one story that Lamar shared with me."

"My dear, you're one in a million. You're so lucky to have found such a glorious love at your age. Most of us never find love, especially one so precious. Even if we do, there still isn't the guarantee that it will flourish, like what happened to Majnun in the story you told me. Regardless, I know that the right path will take you straight into Lamar's arms."

Days and nights passed without any information about Lamar. Zuli was inundated by her taxing hospital workload. Friction between opposing military operations led to an increase in injured bystanders. Zuli found it difficult to stomach certain gruesome scenes. Mangled, bloody wounds and excruciating cries of pain often required Zuli to leave a patient's side. After all, Zuli had neither been trained in the medical field, nor had she given it even a thought as a princess. When she trembled in place and choked back tears of her own, Laily always allowed her to step outside and take a break.

"Tears are prayers too - they travel to God when we can't speak."
~ Psalm 56:8

One Friday evening, as Zuli and Laily's shifts were ending, a woman entered the hospital carrying her daughter in her arms. The mother clutched a bloody hand to her head and dried blood covered her ears. She stumbled before collapsing onto the floor. Staff members rushed to assist them and managed to prop her up on a stretcher. She struggled to stay conscious but recounted her story as best she could.

"Please take care of my baby. Our neighborhood came under siege tonight. Afghan-Russian forces were looting homes and capturing women and girls for their own perverted pleasures. Without a warning or care in the world, they broke into our home. My husband ran to defend us, but there were too many of them for one man. He fought them off while I ran to my daughter's bedroom. The only way out of the house was through the living room. With my daughter in my arms, I came face-to-face with the group of men. They had their guns aimed at my husband. They killed him, oh God, they shot him right in front of my daughter's eyes. Amid the chaos, I ran out the door and took off as far away from the house as I could get. But they threw stones at us and a few shots were fired. I think my daughter was hit. They were distracted by crossfire from some other direction and I managed to..."

The woman and child were transferred to different rooms. They had both lost a life-threatening amount of blood. The mother also had severe head trauma and internal bleeding. She slipped into a coma. It was near impossible for the hospital to treat them effectively because they lacked proper blood supply, medications, tools, and surgeons.

Mother and daughter both passed the following morning. The nurses laid the little girl in her mother's embrace before the bodies were taken away.

Zuli was mortified by the entire heartbreaking ordeal. The barbaric murders were too disturbing for her. She did not return to the hospital for days. On the other hand, Laily had no choice but to report for duty, witness continued horrific conditions, and endure such atrocities – the massacre of the blameless and defenseless.

Processing the tragic death of a father while having also lost a mother was not a task Zuli was equipped to handle. Equally, not having Gulnar in her life felt as though she lost a friend, mother, and confidante all together. Zuli felt more secure with her nanny and grandmother than she ever did with her mother.

Every day, she allocated a few minutes in remembrance of her loved ones. The rest of the days were divided between her work and Lamar. Zuli always thought about him. It felt like he was still by her side. She reminisced about their many conversations. She heard his voice echoing through her mind. At times, Zuli even giggled aloud at the thought of how he teased her. Good grief, she felt like she was losing her mind. Maybe she would be the next *Majnun*. Yet she did not care, so long as Lamar was always on her mind.

Not one individual who entered and exited the hospital had not been marred by the invasion. The hospital staff became limited. Many members of the staff were not showing up to work anymore. Some had secretly fled without warning or notice. The female nurses feared traveling from home to work and back because of the heightened risk of being abducted or detained.

Zuli would have given anything to speak to her father once again. Now that she was completely assimilated with the staff, she learned more and more on how people felt about the nation and former king. During downtime at the hospital, many got into heated political discussions. Two male staff members even almost broke out in a fight over current events. Zuli seldom spoke up and instead listened intently to better understand the mindset of the nation her family had so proudly ruled and miserably failed.

To be put mildly, most people in poverty were far from content with the former monarchy. There were complaints about water supply issues, inadequate living conditions, as well as a lack of both public lavatories and electricity. The list went on and on. Kabul's poor neighborhoods were just as bad as other less densely populated areas of the country. In rural communities, livelihoods fully depended on farming and herding abilities. Schools and educators were scarce commodities, and only a small percentage of the country was educated. Nonetheless, they had still been able to, as one nation and one country, live in peace.

For centuries, if politically incorrect and damaging words were openly exchanged against the government, it led to imprisonment or death. After the enactment of the 1964 constitution, freedom of expression was introduced. There was an unmistakable surge in press coverage that uncovered the governing façades. The old Afghanistan was slowly transforming into a more modern democracy. Yet, political monsters lurked under these temporary illusions. The evil doers detested the spotlight on poverty and favored never-ending nepotism. Zuli was disgusted and felt like she was responsible for the atrocities the great nation of Afghans had faced. Again, *who else could she blame?*

After my father learned of the forthcoming invasion, did he do enough to protect his people? Why had the Afghan nation not risen from a state of poverty? Why were there so many hardships? Who else could be held responsible besides those in the seats of power and atop the throne?

Beloved Father, forgive me. May your soul rest in eternal peace, but I have to address my queries. After all, you raised me to defend the defeated and fight for the oppressed. You told me to never take from others and to provide equally for all. You even taught me to not take an apple from a tree if it did not belong to me. I was supposed to, one day, rule our land to bring about prosperity. But now I know our nation has been undermined and the people's voices have been muffled. Our entire country was sabotaged. Regrettably and unmistakably, it happened under your watch. People we trusted are now saying that their king and his failed kingdom met their proper fate. It is so hard to watch the entire nation drown. I am left with no choice but to take the blame.

Zuli reflected on her father's own words: *Life was a raging river – no one knows for sure when or where it ends, but it still ends regardless of time, status, or place.*

Zuli was never going to reveal her identity. As soon as she found her Lamar, she was certain they would leave their motherland and never return. Who would they become? Which nationality would they assume? A disconcerting reality awaited them.

Anika, the surgical nurse, was rarely seen. She was always in the surgical ward. After many grueling days, the hospital finally had a slow day. There was much chatting, tea drinking, and gossiping about other off-duty staff members.

Anika turned to Zuli, "You look pensive. Do you have information about your family yet?"

Before Zuli could respond, Anika continued, "You're a pretty girl, my dear. You should seriously think about finding a young man to marry so you can leave this country. There are several nice single doctors right here in this building. Actually, the baker's nephew is looking for a bride. My sister knows him. He's the one who graduated from the engineering school last year, and he's planning on leaving Kabul for good. There must be many suitors, but surely none of them are as lovely as you are."

Laily tried to chime in, but Anika interrupted her.

"Laily, you know the baker. He's the bearded man who brought your patient here that one night. And he stopped by again and again to check on the boy. He used to bring freshly baked bread and homemade cheese. Whatever happened to that poor young patient of yours? Wasn't he the one who disappeared from his room?"

Zuli stepped forward, fumbled through a quick excuse, and motioned for Laily to follow her into an empty room.

"Who is Anika referring to? Is she talking about Lamar? Wasn't he the only patient who escaped from the hospital? Do you think he did that because of me?"

What a silly question, Zuli thought. *Of course, he left because of me. I would have done the same. He is my hero. I cannot wait to tell him about my own heroism – jumping out of an airplane was quite a feat indeed!*

"Keep calm," Laily coaxed. "Of course he had no other reason to flee except to find you. Let's go back to the reception area so we can find out exactly who the baker is. I remember his name and his beard, but I can't recall exactly what he looked like. I see so many people that –"

"What was the baker's name, Laily? You never mentioned it to me."

"Najib."

They asked around and, sure enough, another nurse personally knew Najib. He was a reputable man, beyond being an exceptional baker. He gave his neighbors free bread and always offered to pay for others' medical expenses. He even left his bakery to visit certain homes where widows or the elderly lived. He brought them their prescriptions or any other necessities within his means. At least once a month, he went to the pharmacy and purchased medication for the sick out of his own pocket.

"Don't forget about the delicious sweet bread his wife would bake," another nurse commented.

"So, now we know Najib is the baker who saved that handsome and articulate patient who fled from his room. The baker saves lives, his wife makes the best sweets, and his nephew is a catch. Is there anything this wonderful man doesn't do," Anika wondered aloud.

A timid voice from behind the newly-formed crowd hesitantly spoke, "I'm not really supposed to share this, but since we're practically family, I trust everyone here. Besides, we are all faced with the same unforeseeable dangers."

Zuli pushed her colleagues aside, craning an ear to hear.

"You cannot repeat this to anyone. The children would be put at risk. There is an underground school behind the bakery, in Najib's home. Well, it's not underground, and it's not an entire school. Two teachers have been offering classes to girls who are no longer able to attend school. Both of my daughters are attending their afternoon classes. I know they started with just one instructor, but my daughters told me that they've now hired a female teacher. My daughters love the lessons. They are excelling more than they ever had at their previous school. Their teacher has even taught them English. They can't stop talking about his humor and kindness. During their breaks, he tells them all sorts of imaginary stories. I have yet to meet the teachers, but I'm beyond grateful that my daughters are learning. Professor Adir, yes, that's what they call their teacher. And Ms. Na–"

"Quick, bring some ice water," Laily yelled. "Step back everyone, please. Give her some room. Zuli, can you hear me? I think her blood pressure dropped."

Zuli blinked and gazed around with short-lived confusion. "Did I just faint? I am so sorry to have worried everyone. I have never fainted before, but I feel perfectly fine. Give me some room, I need to stand back up and get working."

"You'll do no such thing. Get some rest. I'll check up on you in an hour. Hopefully, everything will have returned back to normal by then. The color is coming back to your face. That's a good sign." Laily hurried out of the room to attend to another patient.

Zuli needed the time to be left alone with her thoughts. While her royal past was long gone and she only had the memories of her enchanted journey to meditate upon, deep in her consciousness, she knew the essence of goodness could never vanish or die. Nothing could have shocked the consciousness out of her like hearing the name Professor Adir. Lamar had probably planned that, if the word got out, she would ask enough questions to lead her right back to *Professor Adir.*

Lamar was brilliant, no doubt.

❧ *GULNAR* ❧
(Pomegranate flower)

A tear escaped her right eye. Another droplet from her left eye. Zuli had lost two mothers – the one who birthed her and the one who raised her through life's different stages.

Of course, she loved her mother dearly. They had never spent the most time together, but they shared a unique bond. In those special moments, her mother had taken it upon herself to teach Zuli the code of decorum – how a princess walked, talked, ate, and carried herself. She had an entire book outlining the etiquettes that were to be practiced to death! The queen often retold stories from the past, especially those rich with family history. She had shared bits and pieces of centuries-old stories about great aunts and uncles who lived the most scandalous lives. There were tales that should never be told. She even gave Zuli her European and Iranian magazines to page through. Together, they read articles on the latest trending topics.

The queen always showed Zuli the latest trends in women's fashion. Her mother was most fixated on her outerwear and never missed an opportunity to dress up like she was part of an ongoing fashion show within their tiny circle of associates. Her mother was the queen; therefore, duty came before mothering.

On the contrary, mothering was Gulnar's first instinct. Gulnar had been present for every aspect of Zuli's upbringing. Gulnar was not just a nanny. She was a tutor, nurse, playmate, confidante, friend, and above all, a giver of love.

Over time, Zuli noticed the abundance of motherly love Gulnar equally shared with her daughters. Although she was extremely fond of Zuli, her children received her distinct maternal affection. Rightly so. However, this distinction made Zuli more aware of her own mother's patterns. The queen spent more time admiring other people and expressing over-the-top adoration for others' children. There was never a sense of jealousy in Zuli, but there was a longing that her mother, too, would have the ability and yearning to love her as affectionately as she did others. Even her aunts paid more attention to their sons than to their daughters. Zuli learned this lesson well. She promised herself that, one day, she would love her daughter as much as her son and more than herself and the world combined.

Gulnar, long ago, married a loving man. Within the first few years of their lives together, they were blessed with two daughters, Afshaan and Afzoon. They became Zuli's little sisters and playmates. The mother, father, and two daughters lived and worked in the royal palace and deserved their own happy ending.

Unexpectedly, Gulnar's beloved husband died of health complications, and she remained a widow.

The king and queen handled all the funeral expenses. To shield the children from the comings and goings of mourners, Afshaan and Afzoon stayed with Zuli in the palace for the first forty days following their father's untimely death. At just eight years old, they thoroughly enjoyed the lavish rooms, toys, and unwavering attention. Zuli played American songs for them and tried to teach them how to dance. She taught them how to play scales on the piano that sat in the foyer. They played hide and seek, colored together, and had even stolen chocolate bars from the kitchen, delicacies that had been reserved for foreign dignitaries.

The queen had been adamant that the girls go to school, and they were given the privilege of being tutored together with Zuli. Children of their social standing lacked such luxuries.

Zuli remembered one Friday afternoon when she visited Gulnar's cozy quarters – her first home away from the palace. She was helping her daughters with their religious studies. Gulnar pointed to Surah Sād [38:72] and read it out loud for the three attentive listeners. After the Arabic verses were read, she asked Zuli to read the translation.

Although Gulnar did not attend school growing up, her mother taught her how to read the Qur'an. Years ago, the queen had gifted her a book. After she blew out her birthday candles that the girls had arranged to show the numbers 32 on the cake, Gulnar unwrapped the package. She was moved to find that her gift was the Qur'an, one that included Farsi translations of the passages. Eventually, her daughters attended school and learned to read more proficiently than their mother could. Every Friday, much like Gulnar's time with her mother, she taught her children to read the Qur'an, and the sisters read the translations back to her.

Zuli took the holy book from Gulnar and read the translation:

"So when I have proportioned him and breathed into him of My [created] soul, then fall down to him in prostration."

Gulnar then elaborated, "Human life is deemed undeniably supreme. Remember that our actions and reactions, how we perpetrate, demean, deceive, mislead, mistreat each other, has a direct impact upon our souls. This soul was breathed into us from His Mighty Soul. To become an excellent human should be our only goal. That is why we were created. He does not intervene. Eventually, the damages and compensations will be ours to claim."

Yet another life-changing lesson from my wise nanny to help guide me through turbulent times, Zuli fondly thought.

Years later, Gulnar had been forced to leave her country; whether or not that was her wish – no one had ever bothered to ask her.

Zuli missed Gulnar.

ᴌ ℒ𝒜 𝐼 ℒ𝒴 ᴕ

(Nightly – like the night)

Just like the night covers all ills, she remedied pain with healing practices, radiant positivity, and unrequited love.

She was often called nurse Laily *jaan*, an endearing form of addressing others.

Laily had grown up with a middle school teacher for a father and an illiterate mother. When she was just eight years old, she lost her brother to the measles, so she grew up as an only child. At that young age, she was left to resolve such a confusing and painful loss by herself. She dared not approach her mother for solace, but her father provided her with occasional comfort.

Her father encouraged her to read, read, and read some more. He was always tough on her because he wanted her to be an educated woman among a majority of people who were not.

Her mother's will to live had been completely overshadowed by the loss of her child. Her ultimate wish had been for Laily to quit school and marry the suitor she chose for her only daughter. In college, Laily found love with a man who loved her back just as much. He was to be a doctor, and she a nurse. They mapped out the rest of their successful lives together.

They planned on getting married and opening a medical practice that provided aid to everyone, particularly the most impoverished. They hoped to have two children. They often talked about traveling the country to treat those without access to doctors or medicine.

When her father announced that Laily had been accepted and enrolled in nursing school, her mother was livid. She ranted about how Laily had to have kids so that she could raise the grandchildren. She pointed to her own life – how even though she could neither read nor write, she managed a home, husband, and defiant daughter, all while coping with the loss of a son. Laily's mother had never been able to move on from her little brother's passing or from her belief that school was wasteful.

Her father always had a way of calming his wife down and protecting his daughter. Because of him, Laily graduated from nursing school with high honors and was immediately hired.

Unfortunately, her father failed to ensure the fulfilment of Laily's romantic wishes. Even though he chose his wife, and she him, their daughter was not granted the same freedom. Since Laily rejected the man her mother chose for her, she was left with no other option. Her first love had moved on and married another woman.

Laily never married. It was an unfortunate fate.

The heartbroken Laily became a fine nurse, however. Patients and their families prayed and praised her out of gratitude for her nursing abilities every day, while she willfully attended to her duties.

Laily still heard her father's deep, melancholic voice from when he had offered her unmatched wisdom: "Your might does not come from just one colossal act of kindness or magically turning sand to gold. No, my daughter, one day I will be gone from your side, so be sure to remember that minuscule acts of kindness, on an ongoing basis, will leave a mighty impact on anyone you encounter. They are perpetual gifts that feed the giver's heart and the world's soul."

Her father alluded to selfless service for other fellow humans – she continually wondered if she achieved such a selflessness.

"The most beautiful place you get to be in this life is within a beautiful soul's prayer." ~ *Shams of Tabriz*

Laily mended wounds, healed bodies, and offered shelter. Her own innate sense of healing proved to be the antidote to her unrealized love. Perhaps, it was the love she willingly, in abundance, bestowed upon others.

§

"From where pain takes root is where the remedy is rooted."
~ Rumi
—Translation by L'mere Younossi

§

CHAPTER TEN
Unexpected Miracles

O ther nations considered it commendable for citizens to exhibit an innate aspiration for humanitarian justice. Such civilized citizens often worked with other countries to expand their ability to aid and guide the impoverished and neglected.

To uncover great humanitarian achievements, contributions of unmotivated altruism and sincere levity result in undeniable phenomena and unexpected miracles. Leaving a trail of righteous deeds ensures subsequent prosperity.

As Lamar spent more time in a war-ravaged Kabul, he realized that the wealthier, more educated people had long packed up and fled. Those still in the city were either on their way out or did not have the means to leave. His country was being dominated and ruled by a reign of terror, and the oppressors were suffocating those who stood for justice and austerity. Although terribly misled, the rulers assumed they could sustain themselves with undisputed power and control. But influence and strength came with lifting a nation from shambles, not from wrecking it. This was, among many, an invaluable lesson Lamar had acquired on his magical journey with Zuli. Here and now, there seemed to be no immediate relief from catastrophe.

Considering the circumstances, Lamar did his part as a civilized citizen by uplifting the next generation through mentorship and education.

Ultimately civility was the candle, the only guiding source of light, for any and all decent societies in the world, while honesty was the priceless jewel of humanity's crown.

Classes typically ended around four in the afternoon. Students in need of extra assistance often stayed to ask further questions. The patient and kind Nasira helped students in need and would review the lessons as many times as a child required. She also stayed late into the evening to grade papers with Lamar. Per her initial request, Nasira was always served a warm meal, which she either ate while grading or packed to take home with her. On occasion, to avoid being out late at night, she slept on a mattress on the floor. She did not want to be a burden to the household. She gave, but she never asked for anything.

To encourage and motivate their students, the two teachers teamed up and created special awards. Lamar and Nasira were both artistic. They drew colorful certificates, customized to fit each student's hobbies and personality. However, the students were always transfixed by Lamar's unusual doodles. They compared certificates, awestruck by the array of rare creations, flowers, and trees. So far, Sadaf, the mother dove, was beloved by the students. Lamar also sketched the lily ponds filled with multitudes of fish. He added a mermaid-like princess blowing bubbles surrounded by her flowing long hair, while a dashing prince swam in the background. Even Nasira once asked about his artistic inspiration.

"How do you conjure up these images?" she had mused.

Lamar could never reveal to her that the enthralling gardens imprinted on his mind were from his journey with Zuli. How could he possibly explain that they had voyaged to another realm, one where everything was happier?

He wanted his most elaborate drawing to be detailed in brilliant colors. He cherished these images with every string of his heart, stored in the special part of his mind sealed with Zuli's name. He planned to gift his drawing to his students at their graduation.

These kids never had the privilege of swimming in a pool or ocean before. They would also never see the rare types of fish which Zuli and Lamar swam with. Lamar intended for his drawing to transport each student into the lily ponds. He wanted the students to imagine themselves within a body of water that was softer than a blanket, swimming among the fish, plants, flowers, and gems. He was going to retell the story of the garden of lily ponds and use his art to help them visualize the magnificence. He needed to teach these traumatized children to focus on hope and train their brains to squash any lurking fear. After all, he was a prime example of someone overcoming loss and defeat.

The brain is so strange. It is extremely durable yet could instantly be broken or break someone else. It creates machines used for killing and destruction. Yet it also formulates fairytale stories and rockets that travel to the moon. The same brains construct fineries and small bullets that shatter whatever is in the way, Lamar pondered.

It was Thursday. Najib knocked on the door and called out to Lamar. "Are you in there, professor?"

Lamar chuckled at his professional title and walked to his classroom door, in the back of Najib's home, to greet his good friend with his usual hug.

"I'm here. I was just tidying up now that today's classes are over. Nasira left over an hour ago, but she was kind enough to prepare us some soup for tonight. We have fresh onions, red and white radishes, hot green peppers, and mint that she picked from the backyard. I hope you're ready to dig in," Lamar said.

"I'm famished. I brought freshly baked bread, so we can cut that up into small pieces to add to our bowls of soup. I hope there was enough meat, potatoes, and carrots in the kitchen. By the way, we have a guest."

Najib stepped aside and graciously invited his friend in. Civilians were paid to be government informants and, nowadays, people seldom trusted their friends and family, let alone strangers.

"Lamar, my good high school friend, Mosen, is joining us for dinner tonight. He traveled back from India to rejoin his family. He's a brave and honorable man. I don't want anyone to know this, but Mosen here was a long-term guard…"

Najib lowered his voice to a mere whisper, "at the royal palace."

He continued at his normal volume. "The kids and their mother ate earlier, so we have the entire table to ourselves." He took his usual seat at the head of the dinner table and rubbed both hands together eagerly before passing the breadbasket to Mosen.

Mosen was a guard at the same palace where princess Zuli resided. Lamar's face lost all color. His appetite took a dive and his blood pressure shot up. He perspired. His mouth went abnormally dry. He drank two glasses of water back to back.

"Save some room for the soup," Najib said.

The two men ate while Lamar intently listened to every word that came out of Mosen's mouth. When Mosen took too long to chew his oversized bite, Lamar nearly dove at him and took his plate away so Mosen could talk without so many pauses.

He recounted the night they had helped the queen, princess, and three others escape from the palace.

"I lost a good friend that night. He served the king much longer than I had and was hit by a bullet while we were still inside the palace. The attack was intense, so we had to leave him. Upon my return, I found out he died, but, in the name of our country and duty, we had to persevere anyway. How does that saying go?"

He paused for a second before elaborating. "Well, I can't seem to remember it all, but it goes something like, 'Do a good deed and throw it in the river, and one day it will come back to you in the desert.'"

Lamar eyed him with disdain, unimpressed by his take on the proverb's wisdom. *Where was Zuli when these bullets were shot?* He was haunted by every detail.

Mosen, finally, put his spoon down, wiped his mouth, and told his tale unencumbered. Lamar's empty stomach, sloshing with water, ached.

"A car was ordered to take the queen to an undisclosed area outside of Kabul. Only the driver knew the secret location. However, along the way, the queen ordered us to take many detours. This was after she found out the king was captured and injured. Against the king's initial orders, may God bless his soul, we were forced to drive from place to place. The queen wanted us to drive to the Ministry of Defense and to the neighborhood where the royals resided. Well, to make a long and chilling story short, nothing significant was achieved, and we almost got killed in the process. Driving around town on the night of the palace attack was beyond risky."

"You were all protected from above," chimed in Najib, pointing a finger to the ceiling.

Lamar reached out and grabbed a piece of bread. He felt nauseous, and pangs of agony ripped through him. *I should have been with Zuli.* Instead, he had been lying unconscious under a pile of debris, oblivious to the realities of a most historical and disturbing Kabul night. He could not believe the king's palace had been attacked. If only his own home had not been destroyed on that same night.

Mosen pressed on with his tale, "To make matters even worse, as we managed to escape from death's clutches, the princess – "

"Princess Zuli, what about her?" The words sputtered out of Lamar's pursed lips before he could take them back.

"Yes, the princess, she lost her mind while we drove towards our destination. She began to sob and scream at the queen and her nanny, refusing to leave without her father and friend. She forced us to take another detour so she could check on this friend on the other side of town. I still don't understand why we were driving around and sightseeing on the night of the king's capture. My friend had been shot, left to bleed to death, and we had been attacked by the Russians earlier on."

"What a shock the ordeal must have been for the queen," Najib ruminated.

"Well, the queen gave up. The princess was out of her mind and even tried leaping from the car while it was still moving.

After we were directed to a destroyed neighborhood, she jumped out from the backseat of the moving vehicle. Her mother and nanny tried to stop her but failed miserably. She fell to the dirt ground and began to scream. The homes there were demolished. It took place minutes before we arrived and looked like the remnants of a rocket attack. There were no structures remaining, just piles and piles of debris. The princess ran to one of these piles and was clawing through the debris. It was like she was trying to free some trapped body. I mean, she *was* calling out someone's name, but it was hard to understand her through her wails. She was inconsolable, and we, another guard and I, eventually had to drag her back to the car. Even though we were scared for our lives, we could certainly feel her pain."

"Are you okay, Lamar?" Najib furrowed his brow and placed a hand atop Lamar's shoulder.

Spontaneous tears welled up in Lamar's eyes and pitifully streamed down his face. *How could I have done such a dreadful thing to my own Zuli?*

Lamar realized that both Najib and Mosen were staring at him.

Lamar wiped his tears with the back of his hand and apologized. "Sorry, sorry, my heart obviously goes out to the royal family. Unfortunately, I witnessed such mental anguish too many times in my life. Your story triggered these agonizing memories for me. Please, continue."

Najib's wife entered the room with a tray of tea and her famous sweet bread.

Mosen was only getting started. "Just wait, it gets better." He reached out and took a piece of the cookie-like bread, *roht*.

Mosen sipped on his tea and took a bite of the cookie, complimenting the baker in-between chews. He washed it down with another big swig of tea. All the while, Lamar sat completely still, gritted his teeth, and tried his best to keep calm.

"After we all piled back into the car, we started to drive east on Nangarhar Highway. We drove through desert landscapes until we, eventually, stopped before a colossal aircraft. Now, you won't believe it. The plane was sent by the Indian government to fly the remaining royal family members out of the country."

"Sounds like an action movie plot," Najib said as he eagerly waited to hear what Mosen had to say next. Lamar went limp. He added no additional side commentary.

That was, until Mosen mentioned, "Everyone was ordered to take their seats and the plane took off, but we were missing one passenger."

"What?" shouted Lamar.

"Not too loud, my friend. The kids are asleep," Najib reminded Lamar.

"My apologies," he mumbled, internally begging for more information.

A perplexed Mosen eyed Lamar with confusion. The poor man could not be blamed. Lamar had starved himself, drank an excessive amount of water, cried like a toddler, and blurted out unusual comments.

Nonetheless, while Lamar poured himself yet another glass of water, Mosen refrained from staring at him for too long.

"Here comes the best part," Mosen exclaimed excitedly.

Lamar could have lunged from his chair and strangled Mosen. But he restrained himself so as to not blow their cover. He sank lower in his seat and folded his arms over his chest.

"With over fifty members of the royal family on board, the plane left *without* the princess. Indeed, she ran out of the plane, jumped off the steps, and took off into the night."

"Oh, my. Now that's a gutsy princess. She didn't want to leave her father behind. God bless her heart," said Najib.

Lamar was on edge. He unfolded his arms and sat forward, clinging to every word.

Mosen elaborated, "She had a head start, so the two guards that had chased her were unable to catch up. With every passing minute on the ground, we were in danger of being discovered. There were fighter jets patrolling the air, and we had to fly low to avoid detection by radar. We still had a long way to travel and the sun was coming out soon. For everyone's safety, especially that of the Indian crew and military staff, they were ordered back and took off without launching a proper search party for the princess. I feel for one of my fellow guards who had to break the news to the queen. Everyone on that plane sobbed and sobbed. It was a night of bereavement and pure mayhem. We all grieved in our own ways to cope with the abundance of unfathomable, startling losses."

"You're lucky to be back together with your family," Najib sympathized.

Evening fell upon them and Mosen realized he needed to leave. Najib invited him to stay the night, but he refused. He wanted to return home before the nightly curfew began.

Soon after the less than empathetic Mosen left, Najib retired to his bedroom and Lamar went outside for some much-needed fresh air. Oxygen was not enough to help him, so he got on the ground and did as many push-ups as he could. Exercise helped release some of the tension that had built up in his neck. He sat back in a folding chair and stared at the night sky. It was darker than usual and the stars were extra bright. From his angle, they appeared to be winking at him. A teardrop, the direct byproduct of his heart's torment, knew not where to land, and dried up by the cruel winds of passing time. The blur of his heavy eyes illuminated the stars above with an added sparkle. Lamar's gaze bounced from one star to the next until he focused on the one that he liked the most.

I am certain You are saddened by what we humans are doing here on earth. I, too, weep for the weak and callous among us. I know there are more charitable and decent humans who believe in You and refrain from malicious inflictions of cruelty. Tonight, You answered some of my prayers. Give me the needed courage so I can remain hopeful. Is it not easy for You to remove the twisted passages before me so I can find my Zuli? Make my nightmares vanish, let the light appear. Rumi did say, 'Doubts and fears divide the kingdom of the heart.' *Dear God, You are the One who could easily disentangle this maze. You could pave a straight line from where I stand to where she now resides. After all, unexpected miracles are possible. I plead and pray that my words rise high to You. Do not let them fade away in the creases of the night. After all, You have said it Yourself that we should call upon You. I know You are very near. You hear more than we say, and You will answer with more than we have asked. Indeed, You have clarified that You will do it in Your own time and in Your own way. Take me to my Zuli,"* Lamar repeatedly prayed.

In the stillness of the moment, he now knew his Zuli was here in Kabul.

CHAPTER ELEVEN
The Queen And King
Of Hearts

"Nothing evolves us like love."
~ Hafiz

For a high school paper, Lamar once wrote that love and wisdom were the true cures for all forms of suffering. To liberate oneself from such sufferings, people must be lovers of a magnitude of tenets. He also wrote how life was a short walk between heaven and hell and that individuals pick up their shovel to dig their path to either realm. Years later, he now found himself in an unpredictable purgatory, between heaven and hell. He suffered more because he had never had to dig such a path for himself or anyone else. His reality had been shaped within minutes. Pangs of misery plagued the entire population. After all, in order to ascend, good deeds must be born from love.

Whenever he found the time, Lamar often took to the streets and wandered around the entire city searching for Zuli. He knew each step led him closer to danger and that protection was no guarantee; he was always at risk of winding up in the middle of enemy crossfire that killed in the name of power-fueled patriotism.

People were divided into groups of conspirators and double agents. Among them were defectors, rebels, and loyalists. There were barely people left to work towards preserving the rich Afghan culture. Whatever vibrancy existed had now been marred. There were no more valuable contributions, no system developments for building a stronger front, no effort towards lifting the nation's spirits. After all, a society could only grow from preserving goodness and establishing impactful, long-term roots for a peaceful future.

At his current juncture, all signs for Lamar pointed towards hell and away from heaven. Lamar grew more desensitized to the fires that scorched every corner. His only focus was on finding his princess. He could sense that she, too, aimlessly roamed in hopes of reconnecting with him once more.

Lamar lost count of the number of times he had visited the garden of Ali Mardan. How many times had he walked around their fig tree hoping that a leaf would fall at his feet and reveal the secret place Zuli resided? She could be just minutes away or, perhaps, just two streets over from Najib's home. His only certainty on the matter remained that they were separated from one another by the malicious hands of the merciless and pitiless.

Today, Lamar did not have time to wander. He felt as if he was on a treasure hunt, but there were no clues, no maps, and no competition apart from time. He stood at the front of his classroom and studied the curious faces staring back at him. With Najib's help, Lamar recently undertook a project to remedy the lack of chairs and desks for the students. The self-proclaimed carpenters hand-made stout tables for students to write in their notebooks atop. Even the blackboard had been secured with one teetering leg shorter than the rest.

Love and *wisdom* were the words Lamar wrote on the blackboard today. The students quickly scribbled them down in their notebooks. Lamar wished schools would teach these two words and their profound meanings. Without either one, the universe would turn into a living hell.

Lamar always knew that one must behave honorably within the boundaries of a sanctuary to remain under the light of veracity. Luckily, both Zuli and he had been touched by the light of love and wisdom, which directly resulted in their unwavering moral justness.

The professor advised his students to take notes on today's lesson, a lesson that would ensure a peaceful future for a generation that had already faced unwarranted misfortunes. Lamar began by informing the children that terror was like a volcano that erupted from within certain, unloved humans.

"Now, make sure you write this down: Human civility stems from the quality of one's objectives, one's impulses and purposes. Remember, the most important lesson I can give is to practice self-love and respect. By doing so, you can all set the basis for a collective obligation to defend humanity and abhor cruelty.

"I want everyone to memorize this poem by the great Rumi: '*I belong to no religion. My religion is love. Every heart is my temple.*'"

Lamar opened the conversation to the students to answer their questions. Every hand was raised at once.

"What is love?"

"Relinquishing narcissism – altruism."

"Professor, what is wisdom?"

"Liberation from pride – nirvana."

At the end of his lecture, Lamar's voice grew heavy with emotions of lost love. "Class, love and wisdom cannot be divided. The two terms are inseparable. Together, they transform us all from within. Once the inner self is cleansed and regal, we can lead a pure life by choosing the middle ground on the straightest path."

The notebooks closed simultaneously. A line was formed. Each student was hugged, and wished a happy weekend and a safe return home.

> *"It is such a secret place, the land of tears."*
> ~Antoine de Saint-Exupéry

Zuli read these words long ago, yet they dwelled in her memory. She cried every night when Laily retired for the evening. She only ever sobbed in private and did so inaudibly to not disturb her roommate. Until recently, Gulnar was the only one who knew the truth behind her sadness. Between each tear, she sent out prayers to one and all, dead or alive. She always prayed to find Lamar once more.

There were two types of tears in the realm of life. One brought rain to dry land and the other brought the fire storm to a green meadow. Thus, the only tears to be shed were those sourced from the spring of delight, not from the depths of a wicked heart.

Tomorrow was Friday, which marked one year since she and Lamar accidentally ran into each other on a back street not too far away from the garden of Ali Mardan. That bemused look on his charming face was still crystal clear in Zuli's mind. She smiled to herself, forever grateful for that one moment of fortune and fate. Yet, she could not be grateful for what fame and fortune afforded her from the palace that stood no more.

The past week had seen less fighting on the streets of Kabul. Perhaps the different parties were resupplying for more attacks in the upcoming weeks. They often moved around and clashed in different districts. The Russians had been successful thus far. No matter where you went, Panjshir province *(five lions)* was frequently discussed. They built a reputation on successfully fighting and defending the valley from being conquered, but talk of seizure was in the air. Everyone had an opinion. Yet, no one knew how the combat would impact their futures. Most believed that Afghanistan would retain its winning streak as never having been conquered in conflicts past and secure their victory over the enemy.

Zuli hoped that, for the first time in many months, no one would come in harm's way tomorrow. Either way, Laily and she were off duty. Zuli had previously visited the garden when disguised as a man. Early in the morning, she would convince Laily to accompany her to the garden of Ali Mardan. She was certain Laily did not require much persuasion – she was already fond of this garden.

By the time Zuli found the frying pan, the sounds of clanging metal woke Laily up. Zuli was not a cook, but she could prepare a variety of egg dishes. Laily bit her tongue and decided not to interfere with Zuli as she wielded the frying pan like a weapon.

"Top of the morning to you, dear Laily *jaan*. I hope I didn't wake you with all that clattering. What does your empty stomach wish to devour? I'm making eggs."

Laily gave Zuli a warm embrace. She neither questioned her jubilant demeanor nor veered Zuli away from whatever she had cooked up. Laily was well aware that Zuli was heartbroken and cried herself to sleep every night. It was not rare for Zuli to have the loss of love weighing on her mind. Laily did not infringe on her privacy and sympathized with her pain's revelation only during the sacred hours of the night.

Indeed, thought Laily, I, too, wept for years when love eluded me until my mind could no longer hold on to the pain. After that release, my mind finally realigned and saved my sanity.

"I'm craving scrambled eggs," Laily said as she placed the cooking oil on the counter.

"Very well. That's my specialty. Breakfast will be served in fifteen minutes." As Laily left the kitchen, she noticed Zuli was holding three eggs in one hand, trying to figure out how to break them.

Maybe her mother spoiled her too much. She doesn't know much about housework or cooking, Laily pondered as she prepared for the surprise day Zuli had planned for her.

Zuli poured her a cup of black tea and placed a small pot of warm milk with a container of brown sugar by Laily's teacup. She rushed to the stove and returned with a plate of scrambled eggs, fresh tomatoes, some fragrant mint, and slices of homemade cheese. The breadbasket was already on the table, but Zuli took the liberty of spreading butter on two slices of bread and had perfectly browned them in the frying pan. She sprinkled one side of the bread with a light dusting of sugar and hurried back to the table, imploring Laily to take a bite while they were still warm. She was beyond proud of her new creation and had even prepared herself an identical plate to Laily's. While they enjoyed a tasty breakfast, Zuli filled Laily in on their schedule for the day.

Before they left the house, Zuli went to turn the radio off. Biased announcers still read the same misleading headlines and offered more false reports. They insisted that people were thriving, and that those who had temporarily left the country were returning in great numbers. They reported that schools were in operation, jobs were secured, children's futures would be brighter than ever, and that the government was for the well-being of the people.

The last bit of news discussed the royal family. Laily noticed that Zuli's entire demeanor changed. She sat in a chair, listening with downcast eyes.

"The former queen has fallen ill. She has been hospitalized and is being treated by India's top leading medical team. We have received news from insider sources that the princess is not with her mother, the queen, and her whereabouts are still unknown. The loss of her daughter and the late king has taken a great toll on her health. Furthermore, it has been reported that the queen's longtime assistant, who also left the country with her, has stayed by her side. We will keep you posted. Stay tuned."

Laily placed a hand on Zuli's shoulder, "Let's go to your garden, shall we?" Laily had agreed to accompany Zuli to this garden, which she had visited when her life was more colorful and joyful. Zuli always mentioned one particular fig tree, which she claimed was magical and made her wishes come true. Off they went.

Zuli wished Laily had never turned the radio on. No one else cared about or was affected by the queen's deteriorating health. But the devastating news hit her with unimaginable pain in the center of her heart, like the bullets that struck and killed one of the guards in her room the night of that horrific attack. The only consolation that kept her from crying in front of Laily was knowing that Gulnar, her nanny, was by her mother's side. *Of course she would be.*

"May the queen overcome such losses, and may she reconnect with her daughter, princess Z–" Laily caught herself and did not utter the princess's name. They already stepped out of the house and were covered by their burkas, so she could not see Zuli's face. *With all the names in the world, still there are so many identical ones,* she thought.

Zuli was overwhelmed with the news and paid no attention to Laily's muttered prayers for the queen's health. She had to find a way to send a message to her mother. They had to know that she was safe and not yet dead. *How will I do that?*

A chipper Laily made her lose her train of thought, "What a beautiful day. Thankfully there's no fighting today. I haven't heard any explosions yet. It's definitely a relief, but it's eerie to think of what may follow such stillness. Here we are, Zuli, you lead the way."

Zuli led.

"If light is in your heart you will find your way home."
~Rumi

A bright light enveloped the fig tree. Both ladies stood back and admired their environment.

"Look at how brilliantly your tree is lit, Zuli," Laily commented. She approached the tree as if being pulled by its palpable magnetism. She reached out and lightly touched the tree trunk. There were no sudden reactions to throw her off her feet. The magical fig tree remained just a tree. Laily glanced heavenward, turned to Zuli, and quoted Hafiz: "Let tenderness pour from your eyes, the way the sun gazes warmly on earth."

Laily pointed to her heart. "You see, this heart beating in my chest is a poet of no sane mind. But it has a sense of direction towards the source of its own pain." Laily rounded the tree while keeping a hand on its trunk as she, too, wished upon the fig tree.

In fear of anything unusual happening, Zuli refrained from getting too close to the tree. She focused her sight and thoughts on the very spot of the tree trunk where she had once seen a splinter of light. Both the light from within the tree and the light in her heart ceased to glow. Instead, she wished and wished that Lamar would appear while they were there. *How else would we find each other? Unless we go to –*

"My dear, do you know the fable about this tree's blossom? It's silly of me to ask you, I'm sure you know," Laily questioned without pausing for an answer. "It was once believed that if the blossom was found and brought back, it would cast everlasting fortune and love upon everyone and..."

"Oh, Laily, there is no such thing as a fig blossom that will bring peace and harmony –"

"Well, I've heard that the blossom has remained hidden, invisible even. Only the chosen ones have the power to see such a heavenly blossom," Laily continued.

"That's precisely what I have heard from those who used to tell me bedtime stories. But believe me, the unseen blossom of the magical fig tree shall remain unseen." Zuli did not wish to elaborate.

While they chatted, she toured Laily around the garden and retraced every step Lamar and she had taken together. Zuli kept checking for any sign of him. As tears slipped from her eyes, she felt as though barbed wires were wrapped around her heart. In reality, the barbed wires that enraptured Zuli imprisoned both her heart and the entire nation, like inmates trapped inside a single cell. Far in the distance, she could hear a soft murmur. The sound reminded her of the mother dove and, as if summoned, a serene white dove was perched there. It gently cooed, as though nothing was wrong within its world.

To keep herself from an emotional collapse, Zuli recounted stories of her visits to the garden as a child, as a disguised boy, and as a young lady who picked flowers, reminisced about love, and wrote poems in her notebook. She left out the most impactful part about when she had been pulled through the tree trunk by Lamar into an enchanted fairyland.

As they left the garden, a man walked past them and Laily called out his name from under her burka. She pulled her burka up for just a second to greet a classmate from college, and they exchanged pleasantries.

"I lost my job at the Ministry of Education. Nowadays, I keep busy by accepting odd jobs, some of which can't even pay me for my work. I'm on my way to buy some wood," he said.

He then lowered his voice, "I'm helping my good friend, Najib, to build a double-sided blackboard. You know, the kind they used in our classrooms in college. It's nice because it will flip –"

Before Laily could probe for more information, a truck full of enemy soldiers turned onto the street. The chatter instantly came to a halt. Laily nervously glanced at Zuli and blurted out to her friend, "Oh, well, it was so nice to see you. We must leave now. Give my best to your family. Please keep safe."

They did not look back.

Laily filled the darkness of Zuli's night with incessant dialogue and an exchange of ideas. Thus far, rumor had it that an underground class was being taught by a young man, believed to be Lamar. But was it him? All clandestine activities were subject to deadly punishment. Was the school even in operation still?

Her idea was to make one of the male hospital workers visit Najib's bakery. His secret mission was to confirm that Lamar was still there. Who else would be in need of a double-sided blackboard?

In no time, they found their accomplice. Within just a few hours it was confirmed, once again, that Lamar worked at Najib's home and adjoined bakery. The door had a deep faded midnight blue hue and a chestnut frame. The house number was 4444. Last year, the street name had been destroyed during a deadly attack. Most Kabul streets were nameless, and there were few stop signs or operating traffic lights. Nonetheless, everyone in that particular neighborhood knew exactly where Najib's famous bakery was located.

The information was delivered to Laily on Monday night. Zuli decided to visit Najib's home on a late Thursday afternoon.

As if Laily was reliving her own love story, she pranced around, hummed love songs, and hugged Zuli every few minutes. She fished out decades-old dresses from her younger days. Zuli already borrowed many of Laily's pieces since her only outfit was the one that she wore when she escaped from the palace.

Zuli awoke right before the dawning of the morning. She pushed back the curtain that covered the bedroom window. It was still dark out. She went to the hallway mirror and pulled her hair up and then let it fall to her side. Then she twisted it into a bun and released it once more. Although Zuli struggled to settle on a hairstyle, she knew her efforts would be pointless. Her hair was going to get messed up under the burka she so detested.

What if she tripped over some rocks and fell on her face on the way to Najib's? She recently embarrassed herself after she stepped in a squelching pile of garbage and shrieked in pure disgust. Those who saw her reaction that day wasted no time in mocking her, whistling at her, and shouting out obscene slurs. A few bikers even rang their bells and offered her rides into the unknown.

Her only desire was to stand face to face with Lamar, but so much could go wrong from one moment to the next. She was uneasy, and a tremor sent violent waves of trepidation through her. She felt decomposed, as though at any given moment she would break into fragmented parts. She detested such crippling feelings. She needed to restore her composure at once. Their fate was preordained and inescapable.

From her wardrobe, Laily picked a deep olive dress for Zuli to wear. It fit her perfectly in all the right places. It had a black-trimmed, round neckline. The same black velvety material was part of the corset-like black belt that wrapped around the waistline. Each elbow-length sleeve had a vertical row of five black buttons. The A-line skirt was even outfitted with side pockets. It looked perfect with Zuli's boots. She gathered the front of her hair up and let the rest fall naturally down her back.

"You look ravishing and royal, like a queen. What you're lacking is a carriage to whisk you off to your king. It seems, after all, that you two are royal bearers of love. Be sure not to leave little old me behind," Laily joked.

❧ Najib's Home Behind The Bakery ❧

"Here with a Loaf of Bread beneath the Bough, A Flask of Wine,
a Book of Verse - and Thou
Beside me singing in the Wilderness - And Wilderness is
Paradise enow." ~Omar Khayyám

Before they left for Najib's home, Laily spent hours fussing over Zuli's hair. She was concerned that the weight of the burka would flatten it completely. Laily sat Zuli down in front of the large hallway mirror and teased up her hair with a narrow comb until it resembled an ostrich egg sitting on Zuli's head.

"Look at that. This is my grandmother's teasing comb. I've held on to it for years. They don't make it like this anymore. It teases the hair so well that it usually keeps its shape for days," Laily explained away while she kept on teasing.

After much pulling and tugging, Zuli finally convinced Laily to reconsider her direction of hairstyling and remedy the egg on her head.

"Look, I have enough hair for two people, my dear Laily. I don't think it's going to look too flat and, besides, I can assure you that Lamar would not care how my hair is styled."

"Oh, Zuli, men notice everything. At first glance, especially, all they see is a woman's outer beauty. Yes, the more refined men will get to know the person behind the looks. But, believe me, it's never done at first sight."

The previous evening, Zuli did not sleep. Instead, she wrote down her thoughts, pacing back and forth from her bed to the window. She wanted to make a wish. Laily mentioned that there would be a new moon, which she made wishes upon as a child. So, Zuli waited for the moon to come out of hiding from behind the dark clouds. A sliver of light broke through as the moon undraped and exposed itself to her searching sight. Zuli remembered Rumi having said,

"Love is a cloud that scatters pearls." Tonight, the moon cast down a simple, auspicious smile.

Zuli made a wish upon the moon as she had done sitting across the waterfall under the willow trees when journeying to the garden of roses. She wished to soon be in Lamar's arms. She wished to return to the fairytale gardens and swim in the lily ponds with the floating pearls. She wished to eat cherries, pick lemons from the trees, and kiss Lamar in the sunflower fields under the fluttering wings of hummingbirds. The pleasures and pains of her life were in the magic and secrets of her daily learnings.

While Laily continued to style her hair, Zuli stared back at her reflection in the mirror. She looked straight into her own eyes, inches away from her. Instead of seeing her own reflection, deep in the irises of her eyes, she saw her father's face and heard his warm voice within her core. Whenever she had gone to The Garden of Ali Mardan with her father, he discussed an array of philosophical topics with her.

From the blade of grass underneath our feet to the rolling clouds overhead, all have value and worth and are clear creations of love. Remember, my daughter, love and peace are found upon the same collective path. One is not possible without the other, hence, we cannot travel this path alone. Survival's sustenance is mere courage – courage to love under the most dire times. It is fascinating that two simple words have been mentioned in the Bible 365 times: "Fear not." No matter where life takes you, go with no fear. Go in love. Go with courage. Go in peace. Go with God in your heart.

That is exactly what Zuli did. She explored the ruins of Kabul's streets without the fear of death or any worse fate. She valiantly searched for the only person left on this earth who was from her past and belonged in her future. She saw so many faces, but none were of the man for whom she searched. Neither her sight nor her soul identified with the passersby.

"Fear not, fear not. Go and find Lamar in the baker's home. Of course, if they say he's there, then he is –"

Laily cut her thoughts short. "Just look at you. Without a doubt, you're the most beautiful young girl I've ever seen. How do you like your hair now?" she asked proudly.

"I love it. You've outdone yourself. It looks much better than before. Thank you very much," said a blushing Zuli as Laily continued to admire her as a mother would her daughter.

‿*Thursday*༄

Zuli and Laily took a synchronized deep breath. Zuli lifted her fist to rap upon the baker's front door. There was a terribly long delay. A corner of the curtain was pushed aside for barely a moment and was promptly drawn once more. A lock clicked open. Secondary security measures loudly unlocked after some apparent struggling from whomever was behind the door. The antique gold-brushed doorknob began to turn. Breathing became a chore for Zuli as she realized that only the blue door stood between Lamar and her. So many doors in her life had closed. Perhaps, this was the *only* one meant to open.

The door opened just a crack, only to reveal a little boy. He stared at their covered faces and spoke in a timid, fearful voice, "No one is home. Go away, please."

They could not blame the child. Nobody in their right mind would drop by a stranger's home unannounced.

"We're friends of your father. Now go and get an adult," an impatient Laily instructed the boy.

Inside, someone reached for the kid's shoulder and gently pulled him away from the doorway. The half-covered face of a woman appeared, with only her warm eyes and her salt and pepper hair exposed.

Before the lady could say anything, Zuli blurted out, "Please, we mean no harm. We're here to see Ad-, the teacher, the professor. I mean Professor Adir." Zuli's voice sounded gibberish and shook more than she was.

"I apologize, but there's no one here by that name. You must have the wrong house," she said.

She made to close the door, but hesitated to add, "Check the other homes in the neighborhood."

"Dear sister, we're friends of Najib. We're here to see *Lamar*." *There, that's right to the point,* Laily thought. She made certain to emphasize the last word as if it was the nightly password, and only meant for this lady, who had pinned herself to the door to block any and all unlawful entry. No one was to blame. After all, it was a guarded secret that the baker's home was also an underground school open to students who could no longer attend public schools.

The look in her eyes softened, and she uncovered her face. "My apologies, of course, do come in."

They stepped inside. The smell of freshly baked bread was embedded in the walls. Laily immediately resonated with childhood memories of the same aroma, from when her mother would bake. A Greek monk's quote, *'Bread is food for the body and holiness is food for the soul; prayer is food for the intellect,'* could not have been more fitting.

Today, for Najib, the baker, the great Rumi's poem was highly suitable, she contemplated: *'Oh what a promise you have made! To serve joy instead of bread to any soul who becomes a guest of yours...'*

The little boy scampered down a short narrow hallway towards the rear of the house. Part of the hallway was sectioned off by a thick curtain, embroidered with hand-sewn grapevines, majestic birds, multicolored butterflies, and exotic flowers. It served as a makeshift door that led to the other side of the home. For Zuli, it resembled an art canvas, neatly replicating their enchanted journey in the fairytale gardens.

The two guests were led into the living room, and Laily promptly removed her burka. The lady motioned for them to sit wherever they wished. She turned to Laily and spoke. "My name is Nasira. Make yourselves comfortable, I'll go and get Najib."

Laily sat down in one of the chairs. Zuli stayed under the shelter of the burka. She was trembling intensely. For now, she was thankful to have remained unseen. Zuli stood by the sofa as Nasira rushed out of sight behind the hanging drapery.

Tick-tock – the longest minutes of her life.

Nasira reappeared from behind the curtain, followed by a kind-faced man.

The man turned to Laily, at a loss for words. He stuttered and struggled to address her. He was completely taken aback by the familiar face sitting on his sofa and croaked out, "I am... Najib."

Laily graciously stood up and extended her hand. "We meet again. Our apologies for dropping by unexpectedly. We thank you for opening your home to us. In case you have forgotten, I am nurse Laily."

Najib threw a quick glance at the motionless statue, covered from head to toe, that stood beside the sofa. Zuli made absolutely no sound.

"Greetings to you, my kindest and blessed nurse Laily. It is an honor to have you in my humble home. Welcome, welcome, welcome, please do take a seat." He released Laily's hand after shaking it profusely and pointed to the sofa. He glanced, yet again, towards the stationary figure. He did not say a word, merely acknowledging her with a nod before promptly turning to Laily.

"Understand, if you're in any danger or in need of any assistance, I'm at your service." He placed a hand on his chest and bowed. "How could I possibly forget you? As long as love and humanity have your kind face, the sun shall never die, the moon shall never vanish, and your deeds shall forever bloom. After all, you're the angelic nurse that gave life to my good friend. During my hospital visits, I watched how tirelessly and selflessly you tended to the ailing and the dying. You wept with the families, cradled children, and prayed over the deceased. I am a man of my word, and I remain at your disposal."

Zuli could feel tears coming. *Oh dear, he's referring to Lamar. No, do not cry, not now!*

The hallway curtain was drawn back just enough for the little boy to sneak a glance at Zuli before pulling it back into place. He was, as any kid would be, curious of the burka lady. She saw the curtain wavering as he actively peeked and paced. Zuli was reminded of her and Lamar's discussion with Kasib at the garden of lily ponds. They knew their souls were bound as tight knots, yet separated by an invisible, delicate veil. Lamar said that only those with inner stillness remained connected, regardless of the veil. Was this the veil separating them? Zuli's inner stillness had taken a leave of absence. She was anything but calm.

While Zuli relived her memories, she barely heard the conversation between the baker and the nurse, and while she eyed the active boy behind the curtain, a sudden hush fell over the room. To her left, a door creaked open, and all heads, including her covered one, turned.

She clutched the arm of the sofa to steady herself.

"Come, professor, look who has honored us with her presence," Najib eagerly announced.

The dashing, poetically versed, witty young man approached with both hands pressed together, as if he was praying. It was impolite to stare at a woman, let alone one who was covered. He glanced quickly at the faceless guest and walked right up to Laily.

Lamar, Lamar, screamed Zuli. No voice came out of her. Her breath was shallow, and the lump in her throat made it impossible to speak. He passed her without a second glance.

"You must forgive me. I stopped by the hospital several times to thank you in person. Unfortunately, you were off duty, but I still left a letter with one of the other nurses. Please know that the mother who gave me life passed years ago. You were the miracle sent to me in my time of need. Like a mother caring for her son, you remained by my side."

He took both of her hands and kissed them before continuing, "I can't even begin to explain my appreciation for what you did for me. The nurses told me how you worried about my whereabouts even after I was long gone. I hope my letter conveyed the respect and value I hold for you. There are no words to express my most sincere gratitude."

Laily embraced Lamar. "You never have to thank me. Your letter was my reward. I've saved it in a very special place. I was elated to know that you had recovered and healed well. Now, turn around," Laily said, shifting his attention to the lady behind the burka and nudging him forward.

ᴥ *Zuli And Lamar* ᔮ

"Where you walk, where your foot touches earth, I will secretly go, just to lay eyes on that ground." ~Rumi

Like the bond of the pearl within its shell, you are the most precious pearl from the ocean of love's never dying motion. Lamar said these words to Zuli in the back of the palace on the day he placed a ring on her finger. Those motions of love were fervently washing over her. Zuli barely made out his face through her blurred vision, altered not only by the forsaken mesh that hid her face, but also by her tears. She rapidly blinked to clear her eyesight. There he stood, barely a touch away, in her domain where he belonged. Zuli's knees were weak, and she maintained contact with the sofa. She was definitely not going to pass out like she had at the hospital after hearing of Lamar's whereabouts. Next to her, Laily choked back her cries and Najib, once again, was at a loss for words.

It all happened so fast.

Lamar inhaled a long shaky gasp of a breath and then quickly exhaled. Like a soft spring breeze, it moved smoothly through the space between them, past the little holes in the mesh. His life-giving breath rested on Zuli's face. Instantly, she was revived; the very center of her core was restored. For so long, she felt like a fish gasping for air, caught on a fisherman's sharp hook, having been reeled out of its natural habitat onto a merciless dry land. That sensation instantly vanished.

Zuli was brought back to the memories and melodies of the birds in the purple tunnel. That morning, she woke from a deep sleep covered by a quilt of purple leaves. She had seen Lamar across from her, leaning against a violet tree as a choir of birds sang their early morning song. Now an electrified symphony erupted from within. Her heartbeat pranced. Her soul reveled in his presence.

Lamar murmured at a barely audible whisper, "Oh, dearest God Almighty!" He beheld her gaze and, in absolute disbelief, peered at her through the tiny holes of the royal blue burka. He could not hold back his sobs as he looked at those familiar eyes of his Zuli. When one's tears take life from the fountain of pain, only then does heaven's heart open and mercy's rain soothe all the wounds.

"There is hope after despair and many suns after darkness."
~ Rumi

The eye is a miracle, not just in its mere ability to reflect life itself, but in its illumination of the soul's bluest, darkest chasms. Zuli's inner fire lit up with a heated passion. Surely, her father could see the beam of light resonating from her. She tried to capture the present moment's miracles in every cleansing sensation and in each invigorating emotion that spread through her. When love's purity is mirrored upon the face of a dark stone, the darkness has no choice but to turn to gold. Should individuals not nourish one another and become sustainers? After all, human beings are delicate spirits, like short-lived butterflies. One's precise moment of departure is a perpetual unknown. What is certain? Nothing but the uncertainty of that particular moment's arrival when our shadows, footprints, and voices vanish. Besides the trails of righteous deeds, only a vacant space remains.

Shivers cascaded through Lamar's entire body and into his hands as he reached for the corners of Zuli's burka that hung loosely over her face. He always envisioned removing the delicate veil of his princess bride dressed in white. But he never imagined this – his princess wearing an old burka standing in the bread baker's home, situated on a street corner by the outskirts of town where royals ventured not. The exception, of course, was for this one extraordinary royal. To Lamar, Zuli was the One and Only's most valuable creation, anointed with the purest spirit.

Like a poised groom, Lamar lifted the corners of the burka to reveal the face he searched for in endless months past.

He folded the burka back and Zuli was revealed.

A weeping Laily took the two corners from Lamar and lifted the burka from behind Zuli's head, carefully removing the entire sheath.

There, her hair still looks professionally done, Laily thought to herself as she folded the covering and held it in her trembling hands.

Lamar and Zuli's eyes locked. Simultaneously, a million longing messages of love passed between the lovers' gazes. Lamar's tears were unreservedly streaming down his face.

"Zuli, Zuli." He dropped to his knees and attempted to place kisses on her feet. Zuli covered her face and sobbed. Strangers watched, but she did not care that they now knew.

She reached down and lifted Lamar from the floor. As always, he kissed her left hand first, then her right, and again her left. Lamar noticed the ring he had placed on her finger. It looked even more extravagant on the hand of the keeper of his heart.

Though sobs chopped his words, in between his praises to God, his golden voice reached her, "I need a basket of white rose petals, pearls, and green leaves to scatter at your feet. Instead, all I have are tears and kisses. Light comes to life and love takes root from where you wander on foot. Oh, how I waited for your steps to find their way to me. I welcome them upon my gaze. In all the places that you have left an imprint to reach me, the dust has turned to a valley of lilacs and lavenders." Once again, he began to bow down at her feet, but Zuli stopped him midway and pulled him towards her. She placed his hand on her face, closed her eyes, and tenderly kissed his trembling hand.

"My darling heart Zuli, you have risked your life to search for me. I know what you did, believe me, *I know.* How could I love you more, *how?* You fled a life of freedom and ran towards the darkness of the unknown. Your sole guide was the light of our souls together as one. You went to the ruins of my home and tried to dig me out with your bare hands. My God, you could have been killed." He kissed each of her fingers. In that moment, he was drowning in the profundities of blissful blessings, yet immediately words churned in his mind.

"Wisdom is knowing I am nothing
Love is knowing I am everything
And between the two my life moves."
~ Sri Nisargadatta Maharaj

How could he know about what I did, Zuli wondered as she tried to cover her pain with a faint smile.

"I visited and circled the palace for thousands of hours. Time and time again, I lost the will to live, but the power of our love persisted and surged through my veins. The hope that dwelled within me urged me to endure. I also frequented our garden, my lovely. Like a dervish I roamed all the spaces you walked. I spoke to our mystic fig tree. No magical voice echoed back, no leaf revealed a message. All the while, I knew my heart continued to beat because yours was beating, too. I only found out recently that you could possibly be nearby. A friend of Najib's–"

At the mention of his name, Najib nodded in affirmation, and wiped his eyes with the palms of his hands. There was an urgent knock on the front door. He scurried to the window to see who it was. Without a moment's delay, he answered the door.

A panic-stricken Mosen threw the door open and barged in.

Not him again, Lamar clenched his teeth and pulled Zuli closer to him. He was not sure why he could not be impartial to that man.

Mosen looked like he had just been chased down by the Russian tanks. He took a brief look around the room, said a quick hello, returned to Najib, and blurted out, "I am sorry for disturbing you. I see you have guests."

He took another glance at the faces. He looked away from Lamar's irate face and rested on the young woman he snugly held.

"Princess Zuli?" Mosen's eyes widened with disbelief "Is that you, Princess?"

Lamar's entire body tensed up. He took a deep breath and held it in.

Mosen saluted her, bowed three times, and nervously saluted again.

"Princess Zuli, I can't believe you're still alive. I did not think you survived the escape. I honestly thought you were–"

"If you say her name one more time I'm going to –" Lamar began to rush at Mosen, but Zuli held him back.

Najib put his hand up to silence Mosen, who stopped talking right before Lamar was about to personally take the words right out of his mouth. After all, Lamar had been a wrestling champion at school and in his neighborhood. He defeated all the guys within his family circle. In the schoolyard, he deliberately matched up with boys far stronger and bigger than himself. Only he knew the correct wrestling techniques to guarantee a win. It did not come to him easily; he practiced his methods for endless hours to ensure victory in every contest. It was most gratifying when he pinned down and held both of his opponent's shoulders on the mat. Everybody cheered him on as he grinned like a true champion from ear to ear. The bigger men did not appreciate someone younger and smaller humiliating them, and they always demanded multiple rematches. His dear mother's wrath, however, was the most daunting, especially when she saw blood gushing from his forehead.

The deafening silence was bone-chilling, and no one in the room made another sound.

All heads turned to Zuli. Najib's son, Sabir, reemerged from behind the curtain and took his place next to Lamar, looking up at his professor with wide eyes. Laily had not stopped gawking at Zuli and had both hands plastered to her face. The daughter she never had, all along, the princess of Afghanistan. Her instincts had never failed her before, and she had an inclination that Zuli looked familiar. Nasira fidgeted with her glasses, removing them from her pocket and placing them on the bridge of her nose. Even then, she squinted as though peering through a fog. After hearing the noise in the living room, Najib's wife, who was in the kitchen cooking dinner, entered with a tray of freshly brewed tea and her signature cake. Puzzled by the crowd of people just standing and staring at one another, she placed the tray down and questioned, "Najib, what's all the commotion about, is everything okay? Oh, hello Mosen, I didn't hear you come in."

"Hello, yes, I just got here to talk to Najib, but I'm still shocked because I did *not* expect to see princess Zuli in your home."

Before he could salute her again, he found himself sprawled out on the floor. The ladies screamed, Sabir chuckled, and Najib dove on Lamar to peel him off Mosen.

Although he was being held back, Lamar made sure his words were heard clearly. "You will never again utter the princess's name. Do you understand that or not?" demanded Lamar angrily. "If you can't get it through your head, then I swear to God I will wring your neck with my bare hands, you absolute fool!"

When they had frantically searched for the unseen fig blossom in the garden of roses, Lamar shared the quote from Rumi with her: *Everything you see has its roots in the unseen world. The forces change, yet the essence remains the same.* While Zuli watched Najib pull Lamar away from Mosen, she knew, then and there, that although everything had changed, the very essence between them remained the same. She knew Lamar would always stand by her as strong as their fig tree or the Kabul mountains. He would defend her with honor. She never doubted that he could be as soft as the dewy morning grass and as loving as a soulmate. With others, he could be the most benevolent.

Well, she mused, *maybe not at that exact split second in time.* When warranted, undoubtedly, he would take a stance of bravery.

Now that they were reconnected, the love from the magic of their souls could move those same mountains and break the hardest of stones. It mattered not that Mosen was sprawled out on the floor; Zuli did not break her look of admiration and reverence with Lamar. He would definitely give his last breath to save hers. She vowed to never do anything to put him in harm's way. No cruel hand would ever again sever their souls' solemn vows. He was, indeed, her idol.

Mosen rolled onto his side and slowly rose to his feet. Still short of breath, he fixed his hair, readjusted his collar, and smoothed out his jacket before accusatorily questioning, "Why does he have his arms around the prin– her ladyship? If only her majesty the queen could have been here. She would have *ordered* me to wring *your* neck. And I would have gladly done so."

"My friend, I really suggest you stop talking now," Najib urged. "I'm glad you've stopped by, but why are you here, if I may ask?"

Mosen felt like he could neither inhale nor exhale, like the air itself was smothering him. Before his tormented thoughts were redirected to Najib, Mosen remembered Lamar from the first time they had met in this house. This strange man neither ate anything nor spoke a word; he just drank water and cried. Now, he was back with his arms around the princess, acting like a predatory wild animal. It dawned on him that Najib's place was not too far away from that home the princess had visited after the rocket attacks. If only that night the queen had known the truth. If only she could have seen this moment. Embarrassed, Mosen stared at his feet and wiped his sweaty palms on his pants.

"I remember you from that dreadful night in the desert, when the Indian plane was ready to take off. I am forever grateful for your services, for your willingness to put your life at risk. You protected my family until their final departure from their beloved soil." Zuli sent Lamar a reassuring look as she approached Mosen and hugged him. Lamar fumed, his nostrils flaring as he tried to compose himself. He maintained his deadly stare at Mosen. *Royal guard or not, this big mouth could very well blow Zuli's cover and put her life at risk. If anyone knew who she was, she could be detained or killed. After all, did they not kill the king, her father? This numbskull does not understand anything,* Lamar brooded.

"I am truly sorry for your losses. May God bless his majesty's grand soul. He was the father of our nation. He was kind to the poor and did no harm to his people. Your beloved mother, the queen, is in good hands and resides in Agra, which is why I'm here." Mosen looked at Najib and added, "I have to leave before sunup. One of my family members tipped off the authorities and claimed that I'm a rogue informant. I must get my family out of Kabul now."

He searched for the right words to avoid sounding like he relinquished all dignity for the sake of living another miserable day. "My dear friend, this is most humiliating for me, but I need your help."

"Say no more. We are brothers. There are no formalities between us," Najib said. "I will give you as much money as I possibly can. What's money compared to an invaluable human life?"

Mosen sighed in relief.

"Now, let us all remain calm. As you can see, Mosen means no harm. Besides, I've known him for all my life," Najib spoke without making direct eye contact with Lamar, who had yet to settle down.

Najib turned to face Zuli. He walked up to her, put his hand on his chest as a form of greeting, and bowed to her like one would to royalty. "My home is yours. It was God's Will that you have survived, and only His Guidance has directed you to my humble abode. This brilliant man has been distressed and tormented by the unknown for far too long now. He searched for you every single day and spent sleepless nights fearful of never seeing your ladyship. Pain consumed him, but with his unwavering faith, hope saved him. Please, please do sit."

Zuli did not sit. Instead, she held Najib within her warm embrace. Through her tears, she thanked him repeatedly for digging Lamar out from the ruins, taking him to the hospital, and ultimately saving his life. She then proceeded to address a shell-shocked Laily, who was still clutching the tearstained scarf as if it was going to fly away.

"Please forgive me, dearest Laily. Although you have been my rescuer and protector, I had no choice but to hide my identity from you. I thought if I kept quiet and concealed the real me then I would be protecting you from undue danger.

You opened your home and heart to me, and I love you like a mother and a lifelong friend. I hope you can find it in your heart to forgive me." Zuli smiled warmly and kissed Laily's hands.

A Conversation To Be Forgotten Not
And
Human Links To Be Broken Not

"It is easier to turn a mountain into dust than to create love in the heart that is filled with hatred." ~ Imam Ali

"How could I not forgive such an angel? A miracle has transpired here today," Laily said. Here she was, interacting with acquaintances and total strangers. She studied their faces closely. Just like her, they, too, were struck by the ominous and dreadful sensation of the unknown. Their futures were blurred. The length of each of their lives rested in the hands of the slayers of life. One reality remained true that each dawn had its own light and color shades, distinct from the dawn of the days gone by. Equally, each dusk had its own griefs and wounds, painted by black and red shades.

Najib was stunned from the day's turn of events. Under his roof stood loving and giving individuals. "Who would have guessed that the princess would visit my home? I do not ask such a question because of her status, but because of her humility and perseverance. She loves a man who has nothing but a golden heart. Believe me, even hate cannot break the links of love. Lamar was buried alive, a product of the senseless disregard for the living. With these hands, I dug him out from under the earth. Now we stand here together, witnessing the reconnection of two souls who were meant for each other. Foremost, we're the children of this nation, Afghanistan. *Proud Afghans!* To have been chosen for this grand mission only means that we, too, are worthy of a safe and fulfilling future. We must not allow our lives to be disconnected. An unpleasant fate awaits those who break such ties." Everyone present inaudibly expressed their agreements with much conviction.

In a sincere tone, Najib continued, "Forgive me, I don't mean to sound too preachy, for I am just a baker. Like my father before me, my purpose is to provide the simplest, yet most crucial of services. If I can quote Rumi, since we all love poetry here:

> *'Passing, passing*
> *The blossom gives way to the fruit;*
> *Both are necessary,*
> *One passes into another.*
> *Bread exists to be broken*
> *To sustain its purpose,*
> *The grape on the vine*
> *Is wine in the making.*
> *Crush it and it comes alive.'*

"My customers at the bakery always share their pain and suffering with me. I especially feel the anguish of those I've assisted before. However, as is love, hate is also a choice. It was *hatred* that brought the iron hearts of the Russians to this land. They know nothing about the richness of our culture, faith, and aspirations. They know not of our abilities, how with staples as simple as grains of rice, we can prepare an amazing variety of dishes. This alone sets us and our skills apart from the rest.

"Indeed, we're a poor nation, but we have an acute aptitude for every part of life. Just think, how many types of grapes do we grow, how do we eat pomegranates, or recite ancient poetry? Our women are mothers and warriors, our artifacts are as rich as the ground under our feet is fertile, with so much yet to be unearthed." Najib stomped his foot down and pointed to the floor, which was covered by an old woven *kilim*.

"Our wealth is our country. We have the courage of lions but still have a modest core. Thus, we endure pain and, with an open hand, offer others our best. My grandmother used to say to never curl our hands into a tight fist, but to keep them open like a giver. She would make a fist with her hand to show us how nothing could be given, how nothing good could ever be grasped with a closed hand. The evil doers, within their stone-cold hearts, have injected our world with despair. They'll take as they wish, yet, in return, they have nothing to give but suffering."

Najib motioned to Mosen. "Today, my brother is forced to leave his motherland. It's more apparent than ever just how much the arteries of our land have been infected." Najib sighed and solemnly continued, "We could very well be on the verge of heading toward an inevitable and terrifying future. But we must forge ahead as one Afghan nation."

The truths behind Najib's sentiments raced through Laily's thoughts. *Once we break as a nation, how will the pieces come together to make us whole again?* The sheer horror of a dark future set in; as a woman, she feared being left alone at the center of this nightmare.

Laily let out a sorrowful sigh. "Here and there, our land is being ripped apart. The mountains cry, and I weep, too. So many innocent people have been killed. In many chilling instances, my hands have been drenched by the sacred warmth of their blood. These eyes of mine have seen their breaths leave their battered bodies. A mother and child both died under my watch. You cannot bring a person back, instead, you eventually go to them."

Laily continued, "The poet, Jami, said that, 'God and Love are as body and soul. God is mine, Love is the diamond. They have been together since the beginning, in every beat of every heart.' When loved ones pass on, the hearts of the living who are left behind slowly die one beat at a time. Believe me, I had to pay close attention to Zuli as I feared that she was nearing her breaking point. She ate so very little, and quietly wept both behind closed doors in the hospital and every night in her bed. She constantly complained of serious chest pain. She even fainted in the hospital when she first learned of Lamar's whereabouts in your home, dear Najib. Indeed, we were chosen to save Zuli and Lamar. They're the eternal lovers of love and peace."

"I was one of the royal guards present when the palace came under attack. I risked my life so others could be saved. Don't forget that I watched," Mosen lowered his voice to a whisper, "the princess when she threw herself on the piles of *his* collapsed home. She tried removing the debris and digging the ground with her own bare hands. Only *she* knew the reality of her actions." *Honestly, what does she see in that guy, anyway?* Mosen kept his thoughts to himself.

"That was the night the truths of our lives became apparent. Yes, amidst bullets and fires were her ladyship's screams, begging for more time, yet stifled by the fear of death. Today, the same fear-provoking tactic is abetting my escape." Mosen tearfully choked on his last words. "Where trust has broken wings, love and peace become wingless birds. We're now at the mercy of the hunters. We can't fly away, but we can move away to lands where safety is promised and humanity is as sacred as one's faith."

Najib was famous for his bear hugs and immediately embraced Mosen with real conviction.

"Please, do tell us about your first encounter with the *princess*," Nasira nervously mumbled, the complete opposite of Mosen's booming voice.

"Well," Laily pondered for a second. "When I first saw Zuli limping through the hospital doors into the hallway, she was covered in mud. Her face was clean, but she still looked as though she had been dragged through dirt. Yet, she lit up the dim hallways."

Laily swallowed the painful lump in her throat. "I told her what my perceptions of her were when she was in recovery. Princess or not, Zuli was still captivating. After all, she is a truly saintly being. With her unwavering courage, she was able to escape and travel with a family of nomads. While people were fleeing, she came back to a burning Kabul where her family and home had been attacked and absolutely nothing from her exuberant past existed. I doubt there are any other princesses who could have endured such hardships and could have still been a true warrior. She is not responsible for what has taken place in this country, but she will forever pay for the mistakes of others. Aren't we all?"

"The princess does not deserve the indefinite torment of not knowing where her father is buried in the land he loved and ruled. It's unimaginable what pain she endures," Nasira added.

Laily took a deliberate breath, "I, too, believe I was chosen. Ultimately, fate guided Lamar and Zuli to be under *my* watch. They have brought us together during such trying times. Our lives have been shattered, but as a family, we shall remain resilient."

"When the eyes and ears are open, even the leaves on the trees teach like pages from the scriptures." ~ Kabir

Laily continued, "Human beings are the grandest and strongest of all living matters. To know this in its totality is to know oneself. To know oneself is to know the sum of all things. The walk of life is uphill. On the way up, tears are shed over spilled blood. No matter, never stop, and keep on scattering the seeds of goodness, watering them even with one's own blood. At times, we must fill the empty wailings of agony with laughter. Each person composes their own stories. Every word is recorded in a definitive book, awaiting our final arrival. Now is the time to understand: we are being pulled by One force that is leading to One place of Light. The clarity of our consciences will determine our level of ascension. Just hold on to one another on the way up – on the way Home."

Nasira held a hand out to the lady she had met mere minutes ago, "You speak so eloquently, nurse Laily. You, yourself, are a born poet and teacher. I've always thought that poets are the most intuitive tutors. I'm alone in this world with barely anything to my name. With my free time, I will do my best to volunteer at the hospital. So long as I have food and water, I need nothing else."

She then reached into her dress pocket and removed two pens. "This is all I have with me." She handed a small sum of cash to Mosen.

He politely declined, but she was insistent. "Take it, you must take it. You cannot refuse your elderly. Take it," she shoved the money into Mosen's pocket. "You must save your family. Our prayers remain with you."

At that time, Najib wanted to offer Zuli and Lamar their own space and ushered everyone out from the living room. The guests dispersed to spare the couple their much-needed privacy. Not a sound or objection escaped the lovebirds' mouths.

Lamar was beyond thankful as he reflected upon the miracles that had just unfolded. In the other room stood five strangers, now allies, connected to push through the tides of life. Long ago, these strangers were chosen as guardians to realign him and Zuli, the devotees of love. Lamar gazed at her, in awe with her charismatic demeanor and ravishing elegance. She wore a green dress that hugged her body perfectly, but he knew it was borrowed.

During their few minutes alone, Lamar picked Zuli up in his arms and brought her to the classroom at the back of the house. Mesmerized, Zuli continued to stare at the walls and tightly hold his hand. The walls were covered in the bright colors of the gardens they had journeyed. Zuli gasped at the sight of so many drawings. She was in every single one of them.

"My love, you drew these?"

"Drawing these images is what kept me alive, my sweetheart," Lamar said as he pulled Zuli closer. They wept in each other's arms and passionately kissed, knowing it could possibly be their last. After all, their lives had been turned upside down within a few short hours. They knew there was no guarantee that a rocket would not strike at any given moment, shattering the house and leaving a ghastly void.

The face of my love is the frame of my heart, thought Lamar. "Never leave my side again. I don't want to let go of you, my most cherished. Unfortunately, to my utter disappointment, we must join the others." Lamar moved towards the door while still showering Zuli's entire face with tiny kisses. She giggled like only Zuli could and returned the kisses twofold.

Zuli and Lamar rejoined their friends.

I had a friend who sold flowers by the river, just minutes from the bridge. His wisdom was acute and his words were embellished, as flowery as his flower cart: "The flow of the river is ceaseless. It waits not, it rushes forward taking with it whatever humanity has unleashed – be it joy, pain, love, hate, war, or peace. Unstoppable, it will bathe the grounds it reaches. Hence, be careful what you feed the river." Lamar paused briefly, "I must have fed the river of life goodness."

He profusely thanked everyone for their kindness and halfheartedly apologized to Mosen.

Of course, only Lamar could eloquently quote and converse through poetry, Zuli thought as she proudly beamed at her fiancé.

Lamar continued, "I recently had to learn that the paths of life are twisted like the rivers' bends. It's up to us to find the straight path." Everyone in the room nodded in agreement.

"Here we stand side by side, Zuli and me. *The unseen path* of love took us not only across green meadows and through desolate valleys, but also through burning fires and dark alleys. Now, we are here once again, and without a shadow of doubt, the light will shine bright."

The two kept wiping their tears, both in disbelief and sheer elation.

"The butterfly counts not months but moments, and has time enough." ~ R. Tagore

Laily cupped her hands together, palms up, as a signal of prayer. "May the light boundlessly shine on you," she prayed over them. "Lamar, the sun, and Zuli, the moon – your glow shall illuminate the darkened paths of many lost seekers."

She paused as she admiringly gazed from Zuli to Lamar. Laily turned to the others. "Just look at them. Not only are they a perfect union, but they are also from a distinct class of intellectuality, guided by their lucid visions for peace. These two are the future and we are the past. We have set the foundation for them to build upon. Many burdens, that is, the duties that must be honorably fulfilled, rest on the chosen ones. Unwavering effort is required to instill goodwill. It is never straightforward, much like a river's swerving curves, but it's doable. Use your inner moral compass wisely; it is designed to direct you skyward."

"Undeniably," Najib proclaimed, and his guests agreed in unison.

Zuli and Lamar exchanged a reminiscent and silent look of understanding between them. They knew exactly what the other was thinking. After all, everything Laily just voiced had the same essence as what Adir, the wise rock, told them once they had returned to the garden of Ali Mardan from their journey to find the magical fig tree's unseen blossom: *Go now! Turn on the light for one and for all to see, from the backstreets and high mountains of your motherland to the great beyond. As ambassadors of peace, you shall remain in the garden of humanity for the sake of saving the links of connection within the circle of your human family.*

"The words *thank you* seem woefully inadequate to express our thankfulness," Zuli chimed in.

"Indeed, there are no words," Lamar agreed as he squeezed Zuli and pulled her even closer to his side.

"Blessings," Najib's wife chimed in, calling everybody to the dinner table, and declaring it time to break bread together.

❧ We Honor The Fallen ❧

"Love is from the infinite and will remain until the eternity."
~ Rumi

*In an old neighborhood in Kabul, amid the chaos, there was a quaint home behind a bakery where hope's light shone in the center of loving hearts both known and unknown. Indeed, they were the chosen – together they moved in circles, down and up bent, twisted paths to plant the roots of future tomorrows.

*The fires will burn. All sorts of footsteps will come and go. Rivers may be parched, or they may flow and spill over. Without a doubt, the winds will swiftly take our joys and pains from here and everywhere, while the earth lays down for you and me.

*Remember, death cannot seize our sovereignty; it was granted to us by powers beyond our own. *Freedom* is the spirit of humanity. Spirits are untouchable. Immortal. Therefore, whether there is one or millions of ones, unperishable, we are.

*Know this: a soul cannot be crushed. Only bones and stones can be smashed. Go and unbreak this world. The truth has no choice but to glow from within the darkest folds of time. You must not fold – rather, unveil. It is better to build upwards and tall. It is best to yearn for love, for all. Survival is a must, the only pathway for all.

*There is a selection of sequential paths, but only a few keep the devil at bay:

The path to God.

The path to Truth.

The path to love.

The path to peace.

The path to knowledge.

The path to unity.

*On the sacred paths, God is Love. Love is God.

*For as long as we stand together, under the glow of wisdom, the world would be a heavenly place, and life would be full of colorful blossoms. Collectively, we must elevate one another as one united nation.

*A circle is unbreakable. Indestructible is what we all are. Reliable is what we should all be. Our footsteps should follow the unseen path to unity. Together, we now must generate infinite ripples of circles so we, too, can reunite with tenderhearted people who share this boundless flow of joy and cheer. Without a shadow of a doubt, you are infinite. Remember, colors create splendor and bring delight to the garden of hearts. Polish this colorful world to keep the gardens lively.

*The unseen path is narrow. Walk gingerly, mindfully, and with a heart and mind filled to the rim with purpose. Regardless of how daunting it may be, walk it. The courageous and determined gymnast leaps onto a narrow wooden balance beam sitting high above the ground. Her durability comes from the will of her mind to flip up in the air, backwards, forward, sideways, always balanced and poised. When she falls off, with no time to spare, she gets back on the beam with vigor and determination. For the finale, she holds her head high, back straight, arms out; she jumps off and lands on both feet, still balanced, still a winner. It is practice and rightness of intent that makes us champions or, in other words, humane.

*Our identities are carved into the canvas of the ether: on stones, on seeds in the ground, on droplets in the seas, and on the colors of petals. These identities are even present in the shapes of leaves, the melodies of birds, and on eight billion or so tongues. Each sin and virtue are clearly printed on the pages of the holy books. Rightfully so, the glimmer of the sun, the shimmer of the stars, and the glossy covering of the sky all mirror our semblance. In the shape of the full moon, in the fullness of the mother's womb, our identities are seared. Simply put – there is hope in you and me, every last one, and every new one.

§

"My heart holds within it every form, it contains a pasture for gazelles, a monastery for Christian monks. There is a temple for idol-worshippers, a hold shrine for pilgrims. There is the table of the Torah, and the Book of the Qur'an.

I follow the religion of Love and go whichever way His camel leads me. This is the true faith. This is the true religion."

~ Ibn Arabi

{Mystic Sufi – philosopher – poet}

§

CHAPTER TWELVE
The Unseen Path

Pain is inflicted by cold-hearted people who, knowingly or unknowingly, leave scabs on wounded souls. To elude suchlike, you and me, let us love as lovers and nothing short of the word.

So long as we are connected by the light and beauty of love's domain, we shall come together as one until the end of time.

No time exists for me without you. My love for you leaves no space or place untouched.

Rumi wrote these pristine words only because he, too, believed in love such as ours: *In the garden, I see only your face. From trees and blossoms, I inhale only your fragrance.*

A flawless joy flows within my veins. This lingering longing is rooted to the grounds of the ocean. It is attached to the uppermost Abode in Heaven, and it is written on every leaf of every earthly tree. In truth, a golden glory, indeed.

From centuries ago, great wise words suggested that one must burn like the sun to everlastingly shed light. The face of our love shines by the fire of our burning hearts. Such is the case with the night's moon and the burning sun at dawn. They too remain inseparable within the throes of love.

Kabir himself said it: "...*What is God? He is the breath inside the breath.*"

O' my dearest, you are immersed within this holy breath, so come and go as you wish. After all, you live within, even closer than my own breath.

North, south, east, and west matter not, whether at dawn
or dusk:

I will climb the highest mountain. I will holler every single
word until it is heard and understood. I hold you secretly,
sacredly, at an ever-unreachable depth.

Your heart is my heart.

I could never love you enough to satisfy my hungering
heart.

What is mine is yours. What is yours is kept within yours
truly. The fibers of your soul are woven in mine, your name is
interwoven in this mind.

Wistfully, intentionally, I am in the throes of this fiery
passion. I fear not. I rejoice.

If I were to forego my life and place it at your feet countless
times, it would still not suffice for a love as grand as yours.
You stand before me, yet I still miss you. Your peerless
beauties are guarded within me. I cannot say it enough, this
qualb, my beating *heart*, is yours. Long ago, you stole it from
me, and I would raise my voice to be heard to make known
your rightful ownership of it.

On this sacred earth, I will lay precious limestones; a
shrine, I shall raise up. Within its rotunda walls, my *diamond*,
you will shine like *Almaas*.

You and I are destined to roam this realm and exchange
our specific vows. Miracles await actualization.

Yes, my darling, we shall marvel at the astonishing
wonders yet to flourish.

At the break of a gray dawn, the sun is most bright even
when the rolling clouds are compelled to cloak its face. Such
is the same fate for the moon in its bleakest night. Zuli, *you*
are that moonlight that lights up such nights.

Never forget, when the face of love is found in the moon,
the moon becomes the bride of the sun; surely the universe
shall never vanish. Neither will you and I. This much I know.

Rumi said, *"Your soul sees your purity."*

And I see nothing but your purity, only because I am your soul and you, mine.

We shall swim, once again, in the ocean of ecstasy, as shimmering diamonds adorn you.

While the sun bows, and the moon hides, I will marvel, adoring you.

How much do I love thee, you ask?

I love thee by the virtue of a most grand love ingrained within my inner self.

In fact, I have carved you onto the surface of my core. My union is with you, my kindred soul.

A dervish, I was born. I chanted your name, dug through the ruins of my home, and there, Zuli, I found the scraps of gold, brass, silver. After the fall of our land, like the mourners chained by their bemoaning, I, too, was bound by my own sorrowful cries, smothered within the confines of my chest. I asked over and over, O' why such a chilling, dispiriting disunion?

I melted down my so-called accumulated wealth and made this band, a bond of love. To liberate *me* from the cages, I submerged myself to weld together such so the hand of man could destroy it not. It is not worthy of your stature, Princess Zuli. But hold it up against the sunbeams, like a halo, and a crown of light rays will forthrightly cover you. This circle of riches bound by my hands was designed to ever remain on yours, a token of our supreme, abiding devotion.

In the profundity of such amour, it is here that I say on our behalf:
Happily ever after our wedded life shall be.

Forever yours, I remain.
Forever mine, you remain.
This is how much I am devoted to thee.
I love God.
I love you.

✌ *A Note To Our Dear Readers* ✍

The section titled "We Honor the Fallen" was written on September 11, 2019. Our memories were alive and inspired by the remembrances of those who perished. Their souls lived on far beyond those of the sinners. The fundamental nature of their evil minds set fires in every corner with a real vexation. Yet, unbeknown to them, the wrongdoers were unable to dim the light of our determination for jubilation. The importance of our oneness has been forever highlighted to preserve the freedoms of our shared civilization, granted to us by the Will of the Giver. In memoriam of those who passed on September 11th, and in remembrance of all the souls killed around the globe, we, the authors, share your sorrows, send our prayers, and ask that together we remain within the circle of *hope*.

Respectfully and Sincerely,

L'mere & Zlaikha

❧ *My Dearest Brother* ❧

While finalizing *The Unseen Path*, our fellow humans were bounded by one astonishing fate – the coronavirus. Around our shared world, we were forced to take shelter. No one dared to assimilate; lockdown was a must, not a choice. While everyone feared its elusive grip, death united the world.

(ʾinnā li-llāhi wa-ʾinna ʾilayhi rājiʿūna)

"Verily we belong to God, and verily to Him do we return."

It is with a heavy heart that I write these sorrowful words: On Thursday, April 30, 2020, my family and I received the most distressing and painful news – my beloved brother, Dr. Homayoon Younossi, took his last breath and departed untimely from life. The virus took my dearest brother as it took countless lives around the world. A farewell was in order, but time did not offer as much as a single moment. He rests in eternal peace within the magnificence and glory of God's Abode.

Dr. Younossi was a proud father, a loving husband, a most caring doctor, a generous giver, and a lover of God, family, and humanity.

He left an aching void and cherished memories for those who crossed his path. His beautiful wife, two wonderful children, two loving brothers, their respective families, friends, and colleagues shall carry on his good name.

Forever remembered. Forever in my heart. – L'mere

Dear Dr. Younossi and I had extensive insightful conversations. I thank you for thinking of me when you brought a box of chocolates from Germany to America. Indeed, heartwarming and thoughtful gestures are the imprints we leave behind as sweet memories.

I send prayers and blessings to your noble soul. – Zizi

About The Authors

✿ Zlaikha Y. Samad ✿

– Zlaikha Yussuf Samad Sadozai / Zizi –

Over the years, I was encouraged to write a book. I attempted countless times, but to no avail. The day I met my friend, I sensed an internal shift within me. A certain awareness or intuition, if you will, gave rise to specific scenes, ideas, and words. Soon after my unexpected connection with L'mere, he posed a question to me: "Have you ever seen a fig tree bloom?" He proceeded to tell me about the idea of the blossomless fig tree and his wish to write a book surrounding it. Intuitively, I knew that I was meant to co-write this book with him, but it seemed impossible because I was not an author. Unbeknownst to me, there was a novel waiting to be poured out of me onto blank pages. Hence, our first novel, *The Unseen Blossom* was born between us.

I am an Afghan-American born in Kabul, Afghanistan, and I came to the USA as a political refugee in 1981. I am lucky to be from an intellectual family of diplomats, writers, professors, physicians, travel enthusiasts, and peacemakers.

I am pleased to say *The Unseen Path* is my second venture into visionary fiction writing, as I am one of the authors of *The Unseen Blossom*. For the past two years, I worked heavily on the novel's publicity process so that it can truly soar, and, all the while, wrote this gem of a book. It is somewhat difficult to explain, but the soul connection between L'mere and I is the driving force behind the creation of both books.

Our story can be passed down to awaken and strengthen one's sense of humanity. This novel detail an invasion that led to chaos both in Afghanistan and in our world, weaved within a love story of two young souls.

Throughout this experience, I am most proud to be the mother of my wonderful daughter and brilliant editor, Madee. She is my heart.

৵ L'mere Younossi ৽

– Khaak –

I am an Afghan-American who came to the USA in 1965 and, to my chagrin, never again returned to the motherland. I earned my master's degree in international business from Pace University, located in New York City. I am also a self-taught man with an insatiable thirst for knowledge. Foremost, I am a fervent student with a blazing flame of desire for uncovering life, music, art, literature, philosophy, and the humanities. I have dedicated ample time to reading and writing poems in different languages, which I then post on Facebook for the pure enjoyment of my family and friends.

I am the proud author of two books, the first being *The Unseen Blossom*. It was born from a dream I once had; I was in the midst of a rainstorm. Complete darkness enveloped me within an uproarious downpour. Unexpectedly, I looked up to see an onrushing object approaching at an alarming speed. I knew that I was supposed to catch it, so I did just that. As soon as I caught the unknown object, I awoke, sitting upright with my hands in the air. Believe me: it was a book that fell from the stormy skies. The concept of the fig tree took root in my mind years ago and sparked a life-changing journey. It has led to the creation of this very novel and the completion of a love story that brought two souls together as one.

I sincerely thank Zlaikha and appreciate her dedication and patience over the years. You are kindhearted, endowed with a golden soul and a vibrant mind. Honored, I am.

↜ RESOURCES ↝

Learn more about the book, authors, poets, sites, and characters:

Amazon: The Unseen Path and The Unseen Blossom by
Zlaikha Y. Samad and L'mere Younossi

Facebook: TheUnseenBlossomBook and
The Unseen Path

Twitter: @UnseenBlossom

Instagram: theunseenblossom and
The Unseen Path

The authors invite the readers to share their comments and feedback by writing to:

theunseenpath@yahoo.com

theunseenblossom@yahoo.com

sunrayzllc@yahoo.com

§

THE END

Sunday, September 22, 2019

2:40 p.m.

§

CPSIA information can be obtained
at www.ICGtesting.com
Printed in the USA
BVHW091704301120
594467BV00012B/375